Charles O. Perrine

An Authentic Exposition of the K.G.C.

Knights of the Golden Circle

Charles O. Perrine

An Authentic Exposition of the K.G.C.
Knights of the Golden Circle

ISBN/EAN: 9783337291341

Printed in Europe, USA, Canada, Australia, Japan

Cover: Foto ©Andreas Hilbeck / pixelio.de

More available books at **www.hansebooks.com**

AN AUTHENTIC EXPOSITION

OF THE

"K. G. C."

"KNIGHTS OF THE GOLDEN CIRCLE;"

OR,

A HISTORY OF SECESSION FROM 1834 TO 1861.

ILLUSTRATED.

BY A MEMBER OF THE ORDER.

INDIANAPOLIS, IND.:

C. O. PERRINE, PUBLISHER.

1861.

DEDICATION.

TO THE

UNCOMPROMISING FRIENDS OF AMERICAN FREEDOM,

WHETHER LIVING NORTH OR SOUTH;

TO THOSE

WHO PREFER DEATH TO THE DESTRUCTION OF THE UNION

AND THE ANNIHILATION OF THE CONSTITUTION,

THIS WORK

IS RESPECTFULLY DEDICATED,

BY THE AUTHOR.

Entered according to Act of Congress, in the year 1861, by
C. O. PERRINE,
In the Clerk's Office of the District Court of the U. S. for the District of Indiana.

CONTENTS.

CHAPTER I.

CHAPTER II.

CHAPTER III.

CHAPTER IV.

CHAPTER V

EXPOSITION

OF THE

"KNIGHTS OF THE GOLDEN CIRCLE."

———•———

CHAPTER I.

The Origin of the Order—Southern Rights' Clubs—the African Slave Trade and the acquisition of new Slave Territory — the first Organization in 1834, and its success—the Mexican War, and the South's interest in it—Progress of the Slave Trade up to 1852—Acquisition of Cuba, Repeal of the Missouri Compromise, Nicaragua Expeditions, etc., used to increase Membership.

The Order of which I propose writing an exposition was, for many years, like the earth in its primordial condition, "without form, and void." It did not receive its present name until about the year 1855. The principles upon which it is based, however, and the actuating motives which pervade its membership, have existed nearly thirty years. About the close of the year 1834, there were to be found, in Charleston, New Orleans, and some other Southern cities, a few politicians who earnestly desired the re-establishment of the African slave-trade and the acquisition of new slave territory. They believed that the Constitution of the United States was a tyrannical document, since it prohibited the slave-trade, and regarded it as a system of piracy. The American Union, therefore, had its enemies almost from its very childhood. These men formed themselves into secret juntos, which, without any particular form or ritual, were called S. R. C.'s, (Southern Rights Clubs.) They had certain signs of recognition, by which they made themselves known to each other, and met weekly, semi-weekly, or otherwise, as the cause which they labored to promote seemed to demand. They might have had, at this early day, some sort of constitution and rules of regulation, but of these little is now known.

(5)

The African slave-trade being contrary to the laws of the United States, and to the laws of the whole civilized world, it was not hoped to carry it on in an open manner. The first efforts of the S. R. C.'s, therefore, were directed to the fitting out, manning, and equipping of secret slavers, which were to cruise around the African coast and kidnap negroes whenever a good opportunity was afforded. Between the years 1834 and 1840 it is presumed that at least six of these vessels were equipped and sent out. Some of them were successful, and filled the measure of their appointment, while others were captured by English and other fleets, to the great mortification of the S. R. C.'s, and the discouragement of their enterprise. They did not, however, "give up the ship" in consequence of these discouragements, but continued their slave piracy with renewed vigor, whenever it seemed possible to conceal their maneuverings.

Time rolled on, and every year seemed to add strength and magnitude to this abominable piratical clique, until the year 1844, when the prospect of the war with Mexico seemed to give them great hope of the acquisition of new slave territory. Their glorious dreams of the growth and extension of the slave power seemed now in a fair way to be realized. In the mean time they had, in their secret juntos, done all in their power to elevate and to continue in office, at Washington, such congressional representatives as were suited to their peculiar views. These were persistent and untiring in their efforts to inflame the United States Government against Mexico and Spain, in the hope that a war would be the result, and thereby an opportunity afforded for the absorption of Southern territory. Wherever it seemed possible to make out a case of insult, it was done; and the most trivial circumstances were magnified into insufferable abuses. Here is given the reason why Southern politicians were so much warmer in their support of the Mexican war than those of the North, as a general thing, and also the reason why Southern States furnished so many more volunteers for the war than did the Northern States. They felt that the successful termination of this war was a matter of the greatest interest to them, and, consequently, were very forward in its promotion.

I have heard a few persons complaining, since the commencement of the present war, that the "North allowed the South to do the fighting in Mexico." Let the instantaneous reply be, "They had more *interest* in that war than we." I do not wish to be understood here as saying that the Mexican war was an unjust one, or that the United States Government had no cause for it. I merely wish to put it plainly before the people that the Southern States had a peculiar interest in it.

The war with Mexico was brought to a close, and Texas, New Mexico, and California were added to the United States domain; but Cuba was still out. The consciousness of this deficiency left an aching void in the "Southern heart," and, forthwith, fillibustering expeditions into Cuba were matured and set on foot by the members of the S. R. C.'s, not in the hope that such expeditions would, in themselves, terminate successfully, but with a view to so embroiling the United States and Spanish Governments, that another acquisitive war would be waged by the former against the latter, and Cuba thereby wrested from its former owners. This scheme was not altogether successful, although it certainly did make advocates to the policy of the acquisition of Cuba throughout the United States.

In the year 1852, the S. R. C.'s had become more numerous, and their organization was more highly perfected. Some two or three slavers were at this time plying successfully between the African coast and the Southern Gulf States, but their places of landing were, of course, unknown to any but the S. R. C.'s. Particular attention was now directed to the ingrafting of the policy of the acquisition of Cuba into the Democratic platform. It was confidently hoped to make it a national Democratic doctrine. In this they were, to a considerable extent, successful; and there is but little doubt that, had it not been for the agitation of the slavery question between the years 1850–'54, the acquisition of Cuba, either by purchase or conquest, would have become the leading political issue of the country. Many Northern Democrats were strongly opposed to the policy, but no Southern ones were. In the Spring of 1854, it became apparent to the Southern extremists that the repeal of the Missouri Compromise had caused a great political revolution in the Northern States; that the old Whig party had become extinct, and that its former adherents, together with many old Democrats, were building up a new party. This was the so-called Know-Nothing party, which, although it professed to be purely American, was the legitimate two-fold result of the entire defeat of the Whig party and the repeal of the Compromise just alluded to. Shrewd Southern politicians did not fail to see the strong Free-soil element which was gradually developing in this party. The sweeping victory which the K. N.'s achieved in the congressional and state elections of 1854 opened the eyes of the Southern Democrats to the fact that the old national party of which they had presumed they had almost complete control, was not so invincible as had been supposed.

CHAPTER II.

Increase of Anti-Slavery Sentiment at the North, and its effect upon Southrons—General George C. Bickley's advent in 1855—the first to Systematize the Order of the K. G. C.—Details of the Organization—its Objects, Solemn Oaths, and Forms of Initiation—its secret influence upon the Politics of the Country—Speech in Castle of a Knight—General William Walker and Fillibustering.

In 1855, it was noticed that the anti-slavery sentiment in the North was growing still stronger, and it was, in fact, generally thought by Southrons that the Democratic party was becoming almost extinct there, from the large numbers that had deserted it in consequence of their Free-soil proclivities. It was about this time that a certain George C. Bickley, who was a native of Boone county, Indiana, but, at the period alluded to, resided in Cincinnati, went South, and, having espoused the cause of the S. R. C.'s, took it in hand to reduce them to a more perfect state of organization. Having framed a constitution, by-laws, and ritual, and having effected thereby all the, to him, necessary changes and modifications in the Order, he christened it with the highly "chivalrous" name of KNIGHTS OF THE GOLDEN CIRCLE. The several divisions of the K. G. C., according to the new constitution, were called Castles. As in the case of most other secret orders, there were subordinate castles, and a Grand Castle, State Castle, or Legion.* The officers of the subordinate castle consisted of a captain, lieutenant, secretary, treasurer, guard, (for the inner door,) sentinel, (for the outer door,) a corresponding secretary, and conductor. The officers of the Grand Castle were the same as those of the subordinates, with the addition of the prefix *Grand.* Their new constitution set forth, in its first article, as one of the principal objects of the order, the acquisition of Cuba, Mexico, and Nicaragua. In another article, the members are pledged to stand united in the promotion of Southern interests, and opposition to the encroachments of abolitionism; and still, in another, they are pledged, in case of any encroachment on the part of the United States Government, to do all within their power to estab-

---

* All the State Legions, or Grand State Castles, are represented by delegates in what is termed the Grand United States or American Legion. From this body all the laws governing state and subordinate castles emanate, as also do the military laws, or, as they are generally termed, "Articles of War." These "Articles of War" require regular military drill, especially in the use of the bayonet and sword. Knights greatly pride themselves on their swordsmanship.

lish a "free Southern Government." The ritual of this period required of the candidate, in the first place, the most solemn oath that he would never divulge anything he should see or hear after he entered the sacred portals of the castle. Having entered the castle, he was sworn to use all his efforts and powers in the furtherance of the objects set forth in the constitution, viz.: the absorption of Southern territory, and the promotion of Southern interests. Nothing is said in either the constitution or ritual directly of the slave piracy, for the reason that it was feared that, by some kind of accident, "the papers" might fall into the hands of the "persecuting government." This portion of their business had not been forgotten, however, for, during the years 1855–6, they equipped and sent out three slavers, two of which were highly successful in their operations; one of them, however, was captured by an English fleet.

The year 1856 gave the Knights a new impetus, and added many to their numbers, in consequence of the very large growth of the anti-slavery sentiment in the North during that year, an especial manifestation of which was afforded by the Presidential campaign. It was now that the rank pro-slavery tree began to produce the buds of secession. Every effort was put forth to test the North and the General Government respecting the policy of absorption of Southern territory. This policy had been pretty strongly hinted at in the Cincinnati Platform, upon which Mr. Buchanan was then running; but hints did not satisfy them. They were bound to have the plain and explicit declaration from the national Democratic party, that "we are in favor of the acquisition of Cuba," or dissolve their connection with it, and, if needs be, with the government. A few paragraphs from the filed speeches of castle C, New Orleans, at this period will give the reader a pretty clear idea of the spirit and intent of the Knights. In perusing these speeches, passages such as the following occur:

"The South can only hope for the real enjoyment of its rights in a Southern Confederacy, if the signs of the times mean anything. Even the Democratic party is becoming Abolitionized. We want more territory; we must have it; but can we hope to acquire it while the Abolitionists stand in our way, and the indifferent Democracy refuse to give us aid? Who can not see that the Democratic party is becoming *abolitionized?* Why does not the present administration (Pierce's) carry out the principles of the Kansas-Nebraska Act in Kansas Territory? Why does it allow those Emigrant Aid Societies of Massachusetts to send their pauper cut-throats to disturb and endanger our people in the common territory of the United States?"

Another specimen:

"We must have Cuba and Mexico. The North is vastly outgrowing us in territory and population. If we can't get territory in the Union, we can out of it. I do not feel like awaiting the slow steps of the Northern Democracy."

In the mean time they were becoming pretty sick of the Kansas-Nebraska bill, as is manifest in the following, which I quote from memory:

"What advantage have we gained by the Nebraska bill? None whatever. On the contrary, we have positively lost. While the Missouri Compromise line stood, we had some territory which we could call our own, and of which we were sure. But how is it since that line is destroyed? Why, before one Southern man can get ready to migrate with his property, (niggers,) they send a whole legion of Yankee Abolitionists to Kansas to cut his throat and steal his negroes. The whole American Government is really becoming a GRAND ABOLITION MACHINE, WHICH, EVEN IN THE HANDS OF DEMOCRATS, IS DESTINED TO CRUSH OUT EVERY VESTIGE OF SOUTHERN LIBERTY."

Becoming impatient with the slow movements of the United States Government respecting the acquisition of territory, the Knights resolved to try another fillibustering expedition. For the heading of this expedition they had, in their own ranks, one of the most daring and courageous of "chivalrous" adventurers. I allude to the no less personage than General Walker. This gentleman was duly furnished and equipped with ships, men, and money by the liberal members of the K. G. C., and sent out to "take Nicaragua." How he took it, everybody knows. But, as in the instance of the Cuban fillibuster war, the effort was not expected to prove successful, but was merely thrown out as a feeler, to determine the condition of Uncle Sam's pulse. After Mr. Buchanan's accession to power, Walker's expeditions were renewed with increased energy; and it was sincerely hoped that, by some ingenious maneuver, he would induce somebody to "insult" the United States, so that a good excuse might be afforded for an aggressive war. In this expectation, however, they were greatly disappointed; for nobody did insult the United States, nor even General Walker, half as much as they were insulted. The only injustice done that individual was, that he was not hung before he started on his first expedition. Up to the time of which I am now writing, the order of the K. G. C. was a rather insignificant one in point of numbers. There were, in fact, very few persons, not members of the institution, who even knew of its existence. But among their small number were many of the wealthiest capitalists of the South, such as Yancey and Toombs; and they were fully confident that the time was rapidly coming when they would literally swallow up the whole of their section of country.

CHAPTER III.

THE YEAR 1858—THE KANSAS STRUGGLE AND THE LECOMPTON CON-
STITUTION—INCREASED GROWTH OF THE K. G. C.—CHANGE OF
RITUAL—SECESSION ADVOCATED, AND THE SOUTH UNITED THROUGH
ITS WORKINGS—THE ORDER POPULARIZED—THE REGALIA, SYMBOLS,
AND WORKINGS OF THE DEGREES AND "INNER TEMPLE"—APPLICA-
TION FOR A CASTLE IN A NORTHERN CITY REFUSED—FIRING OF THE
SOUTHERN HEART IN 1859-'60—PRESIDENTIAL CONTEST OF 1860—
INSTRUMENTALITY OF THE K. G. C. IN DISSOLVING THE DEMOCRATIC
CONVENTION—OPPOSITION TO DOUGLAS—SPEECH IN A NEW ORLEANS
CASTLE—THE CHARLESTON AND BALTIMORE CONVENTIONS—THE
INSINCERITY OF SOUTHRONS.

THE year 1858 found the Knights of the Golden Circle more
highly organized, and gaining wonderfully in popularity. The
division being effected in the Democratic party by the discussion
of the celebrated Lecompton Constitution, gave them great hope
of attaining the end to which they had been directing their efforts,
with undiminished zeal, for the past two years, and which their
organization had been calculated to effect from its very infancy
—the dissolution of the American Union. They had applied
the most thorough tests to the general government, and had done
all in their power to ascertain whether it were possible to entirely
Southernize the great national Democratic party, and transform it
into a pro-slavery engine with which they might extend and protect
slavery everywhere, to little effect. They had proven Mr. Buchanan
to be a very indifferent friend to fillibustering movements; and,
last of all, they had found that there were thousands of Democrats
who would not agree that the people of a territory should have a
constitution which they were utterly opposed to, nor admit that
forty Northern men were equal to but one Southern man. All
these circumstances proved to them that secession was their only
hope. The formation of a Southern Government was now talked
of openly everywhere; every means was used to make secessionists,
and unite the Southern people. To this end it was thought the
order of the K. G. C. should be popularized by various improvements.
The castle was divided into an outer and inner temple; the outer
temple being, in fact, the old castle to which, according to some
changes made in the ritual and constitution, members were admitted
on probation, preparatory to entering the inner temple. The time
of probation was not definitely fixed, but was, in all cases, to be
of sufficient duration to enable the committee of inquiry to determine

whether the initiate was "sound on the nigger." None but those who were known to be out-and-out secessionists could enter the "holy of holies."

About this time it was thought well to do something in the way of regalia, emblems, etc., in which no effort was spared to be "*very ancient.*" As I never had the good fortune to enter the inner temple, I can only describe the outer. In this department the regalia consists of a close helmet for the head, from the top of which peers upward a small silver spear, and to the frontal portion of which is attached a silver crescent; of a close-fitting garment for the thorax and upper extremities, very much resembling the ancient coat of mail, and a long, straight sword suspended to the left side. The symbols were a large bronzed crescent, or new moon, set with fifteen stars, a large one of which was generally suspended over the seat of the Chief Knight, from an arch of evergreens; of a large temple, under the dome of which shone a beautiful representation of the noon-day sun, and around the corona of which were fixed fifteen stars. To these were added the skull and cross-bones. Now for the language of the symbols: The crescent represents the growing Southern Confederacy; the temple, with its glowing sun and fifteen stars, foreshadows the glorious "sunny South," under the benign influence of a fully matured Southern Government, extending its borders through Cuba, Mexico, and Central and South America; the skull and cross-bones signify death to all "Abolition-ists" and opposers of "Southern independence." To the by-laws were added one strongly prohibiting any member from presenting the name of any new applicant unless he had the best of reasons for believing that such applicant was a good Southern man, and perfectly "sound on the nigger."

The sole end to which the Knights now directed their efforts was the disruption of the American Confederacy. Like Garrison and his followers, they considered this an "accursed Union," and that its longer continuance was only calculated to degrade and oppress the South. In view of this object, they determined to aban-don the kidnapping business, inasmuch as it involved consid-erable expense, and required close attention, and concentrate all their energies upon the institution of new castles throughout all the Southern States. Forthwith castles began to spring up all through the Border States, and, in not a few instances, was it found that prominent Northern men were knocking at the door for ad-mission. Whenever they were known to be "good Southern men" they were welcomed and hailed with joy. At one time during the year of which I now write, (1858), some very prominent citizens of New Albany, Indiana, proposed to have a castle instituted in their city, but the Knights thought that as their order was "pe-culiarly a Southern one," it were better that it should not extend into free soil. During this period, castles were built up in Texas, and they showed themselves worthy of their calling, and, if any-

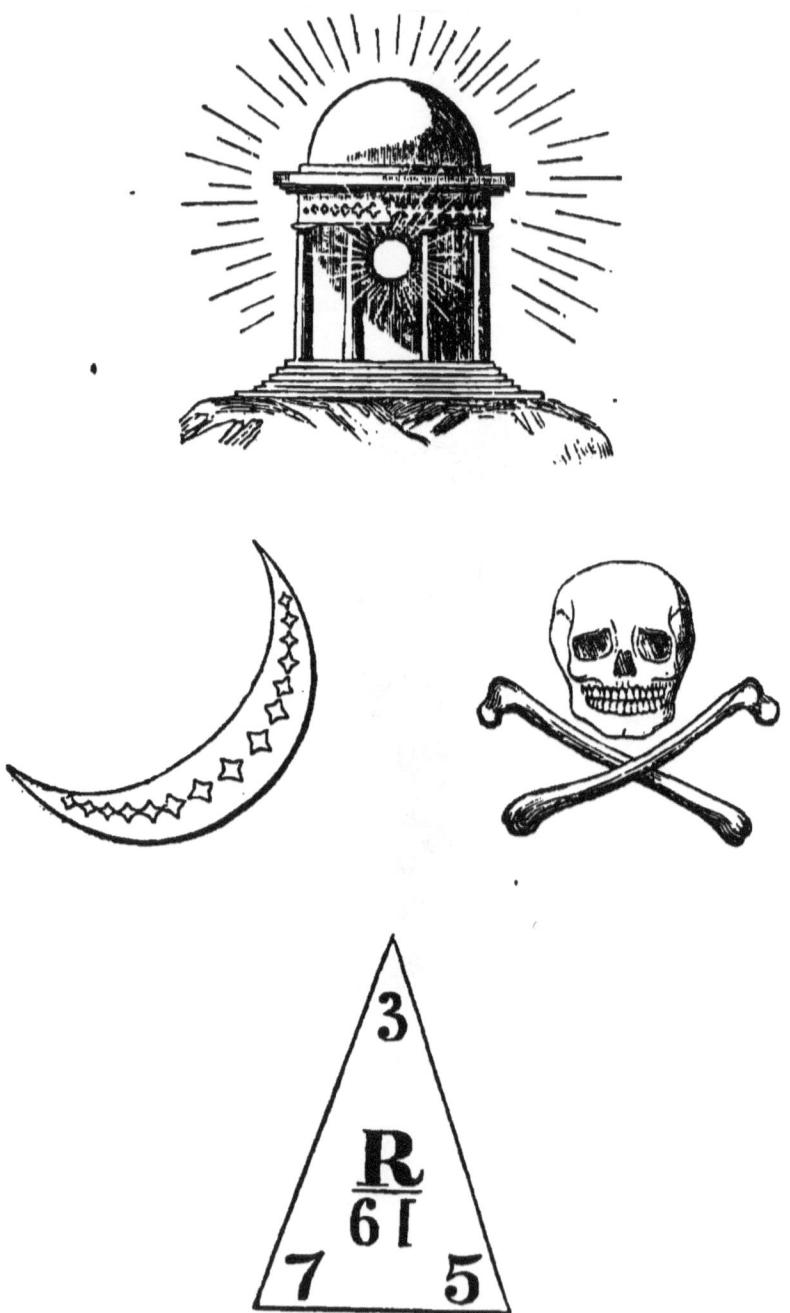

thing, rather distanced those of the Gulf States in the promotion of the "good cause."

With the Texan Knights, however, there was one great obstacle in the way of progress, viz.: the large free-laboring German population. The Germans in Texas had demonstrated to the world that they could even excel the "nigger" in the cultivation of the cotton plant. This was considered as a very dangerous argument against the "peculiar institution."

The great plea in favor of Slavery in the South had ever been that "cotton could not be grown without African service," and that the whole intelligent world should see a practical demonstration of its fallacy was something that the "chivalry" never could submit to.

The Germans had become thoroughly acclimated, and being very healthy and prolific, bid fair to seriously undermine, and ultimately destroy, the slave interests of Texas. Fully conscious of these facts, the members of the K. G. C. began and carried out such a system of abuse and oppression towards this valuable class of citizens, as finally resulted in the exodus of the entire German population (25,000) from Texas to Mexico, in the early part of the spring of the present year, (1861.)

All through the year 1859, the Knights were working with unabated energy for the increase of their numbers and the "firing of the Southern heart." 1860 found them making great preparations for the presidential campaign of that year.

It had been strongly indicated by the Democrats of the great Northwest, at their recent state elections, that a less conservative man than Douglas would receive very few of their votes for the U. S. Presidency in the coming contest; and, from the strong opposition to him by Southern fire-eaters and Northern dough-faces in the national Congress of that year, it was clear that a division, and consequent defeat, of the Democratic ticket could be easily effected, and an excuse, by that means, afforded for the consummation of their great leading design.

Perhaps no politician ever had a firmer hold upon the sympathies of his adherents than Mr. Douglas. Of this fact the Knights were fully aware; and, knowing that many of the prominent leaders of the Northern Democracy were jealous of the "Little Giant," it was duly arranged to secure their services both in Congress and in the contemplated April convention, to the end of so dividing that body that a sufficient number might be drawn off to form another convention and nominate another candidate.

Months before the meeting of the National Democratic Convention, men of the Yancey stripe had literally sworn, in castle, to split that Convention, and thereby utterly defeat its objects, or else entirely Southernize it. The following, from a speech delivered in the New Orleans Castle, will show the spirit and intent of the ultraists of that period.   The speech was made at a meeting held, January 11th, 1860:

"The next administration shall be purely Southern, or we will have no administration at all.   We will have a strictly Southern Rights Congress.   If we can't have such a congress at Washington, we will have it *somewhere else.*   Our rights of property should be secured, not only *here* and in the common territories, but all over the United States.   Why can't we travel where we please with our negroes, and stay as long as we like, without molestation? The powers at the National Capital, under the influence of the abolition puritans, will never, in my opinion, grant the just privileges claimed by Southern gentlemen.   The Democratic party North is fast selling itself out to the Abolitionists, and, from present appearances, we may expect that before another campaign Steve Douglas and Fred Douglass will be spoken of as the candidates for the Presidency and Vice Presidency, to be nominated at a fusion convention, composed of Black Republicans and Squatter Sovereignty Democrats.

"I am, for one, for an *eternal separation from this yellow-skinned, woolly-headed clique.*   I am for an out-and-out Southern man in '60.   We don't expect Northern men to vote for him. We don't want them to.   We only want a man that a Southern gentleman can vote for with clean hands and a clear conscience. I would say, give us Yancey or Jeff Davis.   We can vote for such men as these *conscientiously.*   We don't expect to elect them; we don't want to elect them according to the modes prescribed by the United States Constitution.   We only want to show the North our hand and our strength.   Let them elect their Abolition candidate.   Is there one here who does not hope they will?   For my part, it has been my desire, for over ten years, that the North would give us some good excuse for the dissolution of the Union. We, as an Order, have been hoping and working for a long time for a separation from the North, and the formation of a government of our own, where we could, without any hindrance or drawback, carry out a purely Southern policy.   At the coming Democratic convention we must have this Order well represented; we must have men there who will carry out our wishes; we must show the mulatto Democrats (Douglas men) that we will have a man of our own selection.   He must be a Knight, and a good one at that.   There is little doubt, from the present bull-headedness of the Douglasites, that this policy will result in the division of the convention, and the nomination of two candidates; but that is just what we want.   It will only assist the election of the Abolition candidate, which, as I have before said, is the uppermost desire of our hearts, in that it will afford a lawful excuse for dissolving a Union which has, for the past thirty years, been the most formidable obstacle to Southern progress."

The way in which the Knights proposed to divide the convention was, to require at the hands of the conservative Northern Democracy the most unqualified recognition of the rights of property in slaves, and its especial Congressional protection in all the United States Territories. From the popular expressions of the Northwestern people at the ballot box, at their recent elections, they knew full well their desire of disruption would be successfully attained by this requirement.

In April, 1860, the National Democratic Convention assembled at Charleston, and it seemed to be the universal desire of the conservative men to harmonize that body by making every personal concession consistent with what they had honestly believed to be a fair interpretation of the Cincinnati Platform. They proposed to lay aside all the differences of the past, say nothing about recent quarrels, and simply adopt the old Cincinnati Platform, with the mere addition that the slavery question in the territories should be settled by the Supreme Court, presuming, as they did, that the Constitution. of the United States, as interpreted by the highest of all judicial authorities, was a sufficient guarantee to the rights of property everywhere. If there had been any desire on the part of the Knights (as nearly all the Breckinridge men were,) to forget old differences and reunite the party, they would have readily agreed to this proposition. But no such desire existed among them. Nothing but a full and explicit acknowledgment that "neither Congress nor a Territorial Legislature" could impair the rights of property in slaves, and that it was "the duty of the Federal Government, in all its departments, to protect the rights of persons and property in the territories, *and wherever else its authority extends,*" would begin to satisfy them. Whenever a Southern man says "property," he means "*niggers;*" so that what the Knights really desired of the Douglas men was, that they should admit that no power on earth could, in any way, interfere with "*niggers.*" This admission they knew, as well before as after the Convention, would not be made. Every man at all acquainted with the history of the past five years, knows that Mr. Buchanan was elected upon the principle of non-intervention; and to presume that the conservative men of the Northwest could indorse Congressional Intervention to the ridiculous and inconsistent extreme required by the Southern "nigger" worshipers in the Charleston Convention, was something that none but fools could do.

As my readers are all aware, the result of the unreasonable demands made upon the conservatives was the division of the Convention, or, more properly speaking, the secession of the Knights, and the formation of another convention. Both these conventions adjourned before arriving at any definite conclusion respecting the selection of a candidate, to meet again at Baltimore, in the month of June. On the part of the K. G. C. there was not the

2

least intention of trying to conciliate matters at the subsequent meeting by the compromise of any of their principles; nor did they anticipate any concession on the part of the conservatives. They only desired to widen the breach, and all their pretensions to the contrary were the merest sham.

In the interim between the two meetings the Knights were busily engaged in castle, devising means whereby they might hold the organization at Baltimore, and thereby force the Douglas men to secede. By this *ruse* it was hoped to preserve for their faction the name of "THE REGULAR DEMOCRATIC CONVENTION," and thus more thoroughly divide the party: and it was duly arranged that if they could not succeed in this plan, they would cause the speaker (Mr. Cushing) to "*secede*," and by that means carry all the weight they possibly could with them.

June arrived, and, at the assembling of the convention, the Knights found themselves clearly beaten, as it regarded their first plan, by the superior activity of the conservatives. They even came very near being denied a seat in the assembly. They were, consequently, forced to their last plan as the only alternative.

Respecting the movements of the two Baltimore conventions, the reader is doubtless informed, but it may not be out of the way here to present the expressions of these two bodies on the slavery question, as found in their respective platforms. Here is what the Douglas convention said:

"That inasmuch as differences of opinion exist in the Democratic party as to the nature and extent of a territorial legislature, and as to the powers and duties of Congress, under the Constitution of the United States, over the institution of slavery within the territories, *Resolved*, That the Democratic party will abide by the decision of the Supreme Court of the United States over the institution of slavery in the territories.

"*Resolved*, That it is in accordance with the interpretation of the Cincinnati Platform that, during the existence of the territorial government, the measure of restriction, whatever it may be, imposed by the Federal Constitution on the power of the territorial legislature over the subject of the domestic relations (as the same has been or shall hereafter be finally determined by the Supreme Court of the United States) should be respected by all good citizens, and enforced with promptness and fidelity by every branch of the General Government."

And here is the Breckinridge platform on slavery:

"The government of a territory, as organized by an act of Congress, is provisional and temporary, and, during its existence, all citizens of the United States have an equal right to settle with their property ("*niggers*") in the territory, without their rights either of person or property being destroyed or injured by congressional or territorial legislation.

"It is the duty of the Federal Government, in all its departments, to protect the rights of persons or property ("*niggers*") in the territories, and wherever else its constitutional authority extends.

"When the settlers in a territory, having an adequate population, form a state constitution, the right of sovereignty commences, and being consummated by their admission into the Union, they stand on an equality with the people of other states; and a state thus organized ought to be admitted into the Federal Union, whether the constitution prohibits or recognizes the institution of slavery."

With the exception of the last resolution appended to the Douglas platform, these platforms were both framed in Charleston; and I will remark just here that, as it respects the Breckinridge platform, it had been drawn up in the Calhoun castle, at Charleston, more than a month before the first meeting of the convention.

In contrasting the above quotations, it requires no very great degree of perspicuity to determine which is the more conciliatory of the two; nor does it require a very high development of the perceptives to see that the boasted "national" doctrine of non-intervention, of which we all heard so much in 1856, had been entirely abandoned by the secessionists as a political humbug, and that they had fallen back on the old idea, always maintained by the Republicans, that Congress had a right to interfere with the institution of slavery in the territories, and that it was its duty to do it. The only difference between the Republicans and Breckinridge men, on this point, being that the former believed Congress should prohibit the introduction of slavery into the territories, while the latter taught that Congress should protect it to the full extent of its powers. Does it not seem remarkably strange that, with these facts before the intelligent world, the Knights should denominate the Republican party a sectional one, and base their excuse for secession upon its recent success in consequence? In this connection I will quote from the Republican platform, framed at Chicago, May, 1860. The following is the eighth resolution of that document:

"That the normal condition of all the territory of the United States is that of freedom; that as our republican fathers, when they abolished slavery in all our national territory, ordained that no person should be deprived of life, liberty, or property, without the process of law, it becomes our duty by legislation, whenever such legislation is necessary, to maintain this provision of the Constitution against all attempts to violate it; and we defy the authority of Congress, of a territorial legislature, or of any individuals, to give legal existence to slavery in any territory of the United States."

This resolution may be said to embody the fundamental doctrines of the Republicans respecting the relations subsisting between the General Government and the United States territories, and it will be observed that they are, in spirit, the same as those of the Breckinridge Democrats, but very differently applied and directed.

Now, respecting the Republican idea of the power of Congress to prohibit slavery in the territories, it had the decided advantage of legislative precedent from the earliest periods of our national history to within a few years past, and, therefore, if we are to decide in favor of intervention at all, we must go with the Republicans.

The principle of non-intervention was certainly Democratic; the greatest objection to it, perhaps, was that it was *too* Democratic to be applied to this age and this Government.

One of the principal causes of the destruction of the Grecian Republic was, that its Democracy was in advance of the intelligence of its people; and it may be that, of late years, some of our American statesmen have, in their ambitious desire to attract the attention of the world and leave their mark upon the times, which, under ordinary circumstances, is commendable, endeavored to lead this nation beyond the capacity of its sovereigns.

CHAPTER IV.

THE CONTEST OF 1860—THE BRECKINRIDGE MOVEMENT, AND THE
INSINCERITY OF ITS OPPOSITION TO LINCOLN—THE K. G. C. AT THE
NORTH AND THE SOUTH—MISREPRESENTATIONS BY NORTHERN
KNIGHTS—SOME OF THEIR BOASTING LETTERS—AID EXPECTED FROM
THE NORTH IN CASE OF SECESSION—NEW EMBLEM OF THE ORDER
—PLANS TO STEAL ARMS AND MONEY FROM THE U. S. MATURED IN
CASTLE IN 1859—LINCOLN AND HAMLIN SCARECROW AT THE SOUTH
—STORIES OF THE CAMPAIGN, AND THEIR ALMOST GENERAL BELIEF
—TREATMENT OF NORTHERNERS AT THE SOUTH.

THE two Baltimore Conventions having finished their work,
adjourned, and went forth organizing state tickets, and presenting
the claims of their respective candidates to the people of the country.
Now, be it remembered, there were many warm supporters of Mr.
Buchanan's administration, and political enemies of Senator Douglas,
who, seeing the disorganized condition of the Democratic party,
and the certain prospect of defeat in consequence, were willing to
make almost any personal sacrifice in order to bring about a better
state of affairs. These proposed to allow Breckinridge to take the
South and Douglas the North, in the hope that thereby the election
of Lincoln would be prevented, and the choice thrown into Congress.
These men were honest in their intentions, whatever we may say
of their political views. They labored earnestly to prevent the
organization of a Breckinridge ticket in any Northern State; but
they were not members of the K. G. C., and, consequently, unacquainted with the real intent and meaning of the Breckinridge
movement. Their reasoning, their efforts, their appeals, were not
heeded, and almost before we were aware of it, there was a Secession
ticket (that is the proper name) in nearly every state north of the
Ohio River, with such men as the Hon. J. D. B—— and D. S. D——
to stump for it, and such papers as the *New York Day Book* to talk
for it. There were many men in the North who were not bona-fide
members of the K. G. C., who still advocated the claim of the
Secession ticket almost purely out of the hatred and envy they
bore Mr. Douglas; others again were duped and lured into it. A
certain Mr. B——, of Indiana, a Mr. V——, of Ohio, the editor
of the *Day Book*, and a Mr. C——, of Massachusetts, were said to
be about the only reliable members the Order claimed among the
prominent Northern politicians. Of course there were several of the
"small fry" in many places. It was frequently wondered why any
set of men could be so foolish as to advocate the Breckinridge ticket
in the North, and often the questions were asked, "Why do you

do it?"—" What will you make by it?" The reply generally was, " We hope to make nothing; we act from principle." With some, these answers were, doubtless, honest, inasmuch as they were ignorant of the operations and intentions of the Knights in the South, who were, as I have just shown, at the bottom of the whole movement.

As has already been seen, the members of the K. G. C. hoped by the organization of the Secession ticket in the North, to more effectually divide the Democratic party. But there was with them another and far greater object to be attained by it, viz.: the ascertainment of the precise number of Northern men with decided Southern principles. This was a desideratum of no little importance, since it was honestly believed and fully expected that, in the pending revolution of 1861, every man in the North who had voted for Breckinridge might be set down on the lists as a soldier for the Southern army. All over the North agents were employed to attend the elections, ascertain the exact number of Breckinridge voters, and forward the same to any regularly organized castle in the South. This latter movement was somewhat interrupted in New York and some other Eastern states by the Union coalition entered into by all the parties opposed to the election of Mr. Lincoln. But, notwithstanding this, a pretty accurate calculation was made of the probable sympathetic aid that might be expected from every state north of Mason and Dixon's line. About two months before the presidential election, there was an extensive correspondence going on between Northern and Southern Knights, in which the former were representing the secession strength of their section as being very great. In this connection I have thought fit to present, in substance, a few letters which I have had the opportunity of seeing. If I had been safe in so doing, I would have copied them verbatim.

Here is one written from Madison, Indiana:

MADISON, Sept. —, 1860.
CORRESPONDING SEC. JEFFERSON CASTLE, No. 23, K. G. C.
Dear Sir:—You may tell the friends of Southern Rights that our district can turn out at least one thousand men who will fight Northern aggression to the death. Be of good cheer, and work faithfully.
Yours for the right,   T.

The following is the substance of an epistle written from Evansville, Indiana:

EVANSVILLE, Sept. —, 1860.
CORRESPONDING SEC. JEFFERSON CASTLE, K. G. C.
Dear Sir:—Tell the friends that our county, alone, will be found good for one regiment of brave men, who will shed their last drop of blood before they will submit to Abolition rule. Put us down as A, number one.   Very respectfully yours, etc.,   S.

Washington, Indiana, is heard from in the following manner:

WASHINGTON, IND., Sept. —, 1860.

CORRESPONDING SEC. JEFF. CASTLE, K. G. C.

Dear Sir :—Having been generally over the Hoosier State, I think I can tell pretty accurately how she stands. There are thirty thousand voters in this State who will never compromise with Black Republicanism, and I think I may safely say that there are at least ten thousand who will shoulder their muskets in defense of the rights of their Southern brethren. Your ob't servant, M.

The letter below is from the little town of Carlisle, Indiana:

CARLISLE, Sept. —, 1860.

CORRESPONDING SEC. JEFFERSON CASTLE, K. G. C.

Dear Sir :—I have taken the pains to count noses in this district, especially in this county, and I can set you down, at the least calculation, two thousand fighting men, who will, at a moment's warning, in case of need, march to the standard of Southern Rights, and it is highly probable that the whole of Indiana south of the National Road will secede and unite its fortune with the South when Lincoln is elected. Ever yours, etc., W.

The foregoing letters I saw and read among the filed papers of Jefferson Castle, Kentucky, and these were from Indiana alone. From what I could gather from prominent members of the Order, I think I may safely estimate the promised sympathetic aid of the several Northwestern States as follows: Indiana, at least 10,000; Ohio, about 5,000; Illinois, 5,000; Pennsylvania, at least 15,000; New York, about 50,000; Iowa, 5,000; Michigan, 5,000. Total, 95,000. Beside the assistance expected from the above mentioned States, they looked for a good deal from others, both in the way of men and money. At no time previous to the bombardment of Fort Sumter was it presumed that the number of men to be counted on from the North would fall below 100,000, and with these, and the assistance of Northern capitalists, Northern engineers, manufacturers, etc., together with the heavy drafts to be made on the U. S. Treasury and the U. S. Arsenals, it was confidently apprehended as nothing more than a breakfast spell to "*clean out the Abolitionists*," capture the Capital at Washington, and kick Uncle Sam into nonenity.

About this time a new emblem was added to the Order. It was a simple triangular white card, somewhat resembling the Knights' spear, in the three corners of which were written the figures 7, 3, and 5. In the center of this card was printed the capital letter R, and immediately below this was written the number 61. Let the reader presume this card to be placed before him with the long, acute angle upward, as the upper part of a spear *in situ;* let him imagine the figure 7 in the left hand corner, the figure 3 in the upper corner, and the figure 5 in the right hand corner. Now he should place the capital letter R in the center of the card, and

61 immediately under it, and read as follows, beginning with the capital R., and running round the several angles of the card, from left to right: R.—Revolution. 7-3-5=15, of fifteen states in '61, (1861,) or Revolution of fifteen states in sixty-one. These cards were thrown about the streets and corners of many of the Northern border cities nearly two months before the election of Mr. Lincoln.

I have already intimated that secret arrangements had been made to secure a considerable portion of Uncle Sam's money at this period. This is true. Floyd and Cobb had taken all the necessary preliminary steps for the accomplishment of this object nearly two years previous to the time of which I am now writing. Plans for securing the arms of U. S. Arsenals, and possessing all the Southern fortresses, had been thoroughly matured about one year previous, historical evidence of which is presented in succeeding pages of this work. In addition to the foregoing, by far the larger portion of the regular army had been distributed among various outposts in Texas and Utah, where it was quite out of reach. The Navy had been, with the exception of an insignificant home squadron, sent to the most distant foreign points by that poor, pitiful, *nigger truckling* yankee, Isaac Toucey, in order that it might not be readily recalled. Further, it was arranged to send nearly every navy officer of known loyalty abroad, while a large majority of those to be selected for the home squadron were Knights of the genuine stamp. To Delaware, Maryland, Virginia, Kentucky, Tennessee, Arkansas, and Missouri, where it was known that the K. G. C. were vastly in the minority, no arms were to be distributed, or at least as few as possible, whereas in the Cotton States, where the Order was pretty strong, and where its members generally managed, by hook or crook, to be at the head of all public affairs, large numbers were sent. In order to more thoroughly prepare the people of the Gulf States for the anticipated revolution, it was resolved upon to use every means to make them believe that if Mr. Lincoln was elected, the almost immediate abolition of slavery in all the Slave States would follow; and that he (Lincoln) was, in point of civilization, but a few removes from a Fejee Islander. The newspapers under the control of the Knights were constantly employed in giving the most distorted and unjust delineations of the characters of the Republican nominees. Northern editors who wrote disparagingly or abusively of Lincoln and the Republican party were largely quoted from, and in small country sheets which rarely ever reached a Northern or border town, such quotations were miserably garbled, and presented to the people vastly more unjust than they were originally. In many of the Gulf States the common people were fully of the opinion that Mr. Hamlin was a mulatto, from the newspaper descriptions they had read of him. Mr. Lincoln was generally believed to be a totally illiterate numskull, as barbarous toward the Southern slaveholders as a Hottentot, and as dear a lover of 'niggers" as a German is of lager beer. It was even currently reported, at one time, that his wife was a quadroon.

Meantime, such a course was to be pursued toward Northern men caught in the South, of the slightest Republican tendency, as would stir up the indignation of the Northern people. Men were to be tarred and feathered, ridden on rails, ducked in muddy water, and even hung, or shot, where any sufficient excuse could be had. In short, every species of taunt and insult were to be used in order to arouse and irritate the North, so that Mr. Lincoln's election might be all the more certain. The effects of ruffianism in Kansas had proven to them that the more they abused the North, the more intense would be its opposition to that institution which really does seem to engender, either directly or indirectly, more grossness and brutality than almost any other known to the civilized world. Just here I might relate a few incidents which occurred a short time before the Presidential election, which fully illustrate the truth of what I have just been stating. In Nashville, Tenn., about the middle of September, 1860, there were found, wrapped around some books, a few copies of the N. Y. Tribune, in the trunk of a gentleman from Boston, who had been teaching music in Nashville nearly two years. The mere finding of these papers in his possession was construed by Knights into "distributing incendiary documents." His conviction having been fully established by this mere fact, he was conveyed to a duck puddle and thoroughly soaked in its muddy contents; he was then *gently* tarred and feathered, ridden on a rail all around town, followed by a gang of the "chivalry," and finally driven out of town by the locomotive "property" which it was thought his two year old Tribunes were likely to injure. Another instance. An "Egyptian," from Illinois, who had been on a visit to some of his friends in Tennessee, in September, 1860, and who had been born and raised in that state, was going home per railroad through Kentucky. The train was pretty well filled with Knights on their way to Louisville, to assist in organizing a new castle in that place. Perceiving, from his appearance, that he was a Northerner, they proceeded to cross-examine the "Egyptian" respecting his politics. Seeing, from the complexion of things that the surrounding atmosphere was highly "chivalrous," and not being as successful a hypocrite as the "Subscriber," he endeavored to pursue the non-committal course. But that would not do; they only persisted the more urgently with their quizzings. Finally, he told them, very frankly, that if he must come out, he expected to vote for "Old Abe," if he lived till the coming election. This acknowledgment was the signal for hisses, groanings, jeerings, etc., and finally one of the crowd attempted to pull his nose, when he pulled off his coat, drew himself up *a la* Heenan, and swore most lustily that if they undertook anything of that kind, he would "thrash the whole d—d car load." Fortunately, the conductor, and one or two other genuine Kentucky gentlemen, induced the K. G. C.'s to desist their more than heathenish conduct. But still they could not give the job up entirely; and when the train stopped at the next station, they induced the women and children from the adjoining cars to come in and look at what they called the "*Lincoln animal.*" I did not learn whether they charged an admission fee at the door, but understood that many of the "young 'uns" considered it a very rare exhibition.

And still another case: Judge ——, of Greencastle, Ind., was visiting some relatives in the western part of Kentucky, in the latter part of September, 1860, and being on a train one day which contained a goodly number of the "chivalry," was questioned by them very closely as to his politics. He told them he was a Lincoln man, when several of them began to curse him, and threaten to put him off the train. The Judge, however, showed them his mettle, gave them to understand that he, too, was a Kentuckian by nativity, and that before they insulted him they had to do some hard fighting. They concluded to let him alone.

Many instances more of a similar and even worse character could be adduced to the point, but these are sufficient to give the reader some idea of the Knights' tactics towards Northern men in the fall of 1860. During the whole of Lincoln's campaign, the newspapers were full of accounts of almost insufferable abuses received by Northern men, every one of which was justly attributable to the Knights. It is but justice to the South, however, to state that there were, at this time, many Southern gentlemen, even of the strong pro-slavery stamp, who utterly discountenanced these outrages.

CHAPTER V.

The close of Lincoln's Campaign—"Submissionists"—"Firing the Southern Heart" for Secession—Great Increase of the Knighthood—New Degrees instituted—the Sworn Brotherhood pledged to a Southern Government—Death of Abolitionists and other Crimes licensed—the Election of Lincoln a plea for "Southern Deliverance"—Charleston Castle—the "Cockade" excitement—Joy over the Election of Lincoln—"Co-operationists" confounded by the "Precipitators"—Immediate Secession the war-cry of the K. G. C.—the Secession of South Carolina, and its Effect upon the Gulf States—the K. G. C. opposed to Compromises—the Different Modes of Adjustment proposed in Congress hooted at.

Toward the close of Mr. Lincoln's campaign it became apparent that his election was pretty certain. Nearly all the great Middle and Northwestern States had elected the Republican state ticket, and it now seemed that the grand object for which the Knights had labored so earnestly was about to be attained. In view of this contingency, they adopted a regular system of brow-beating, almost unequaled in the history of the world. They coined the appellation "Submissionist," and applied it, with great bitterness, to every man who indicated that he would await the committal of some overt act before he was willing his state should go out of the Union. Every editor and orator under their control, or within their hellish precincts, indulged in the most abusive epithets toward loyal citizens. Every appeal was made to Southern pride and Southern honor. Full well they knew the effects of this system of "coercing" the Southern people into the inextricable vortex of secession. Almost any really high-toned gentleman of the South prefers death to the name "*coward*," which term was considered by the "chivalry" as synonymous with "Submissionist." This devilish, domineering, and yet cowardly style of "firing the Southern heart," did more to induce men to enlist in the cause of secession than any other that could have been adopted.

Further, it was now considered a good time to extend the Order of the K. G. C. Every man among them, therefore, who had education enough to read the ritual, was delegated to go forth and organize castles wherever he could find the material with which to construct one. In drumming for the Order, the agents took care to say nothing about the original objects for which it was framed, viz.: the re-establishment of the African slave-trade and the acquisition of slave territory. It was always represented to outsiders as a strictly "anti-submission" Order, only designed to aid in the securing of "Southern rights;" and of course almost every Southern man is for Southern rights. Castles were organized wherever a sufficient number could be got together for the purpose, irrespective of regalia, emblems, or any of the regular paraphernalia of the Order. Court-rooms, store-rooms, and even smoke-houses and stables were used. New degrees were instituted, which were called "preliminary" degrees. In these the candidate saw but little of the "inner beauties" of the castle. In the first, he was only sworn to resist the encroachments of "abolitionism" with all his powers; in the second, he was sworn to stand by the South, and especially his own state, and follow her destinies, wherever they tended; in the third, which was the last of the "preliminary" degrees, he was obligated to favor a Southern Confederacy, and to pledge himself, and all that he had, in its support, when it should be formed. The candidate was now prepared to enter the Outer Temple of the castle, where he was received according to the new ritual, (one framed and adopted in October, 1860,) which required the most solemn pledges that the initiate would never retrace a single one of his recent steps, and that he would, to the utmost of his powers, aid in promoting the formation of a Southern government. Further, this ritual demands that a man shall consider no act toward the enemies of "Southern rights" as too gross or unjust for him to commit. In other words, he is required to swear that he will do anything to punish "Abolitionists" and bring them to terms, the injury of their women and children excepted. This last feature, viz.: the exception, is really the only redeeming one of the whole affair. This ritual also gives the initiate license to kill any man whom he has reason to believe is a real Abolitionist, in any way he sees proper, and the Order is pledged to protect him to the end.

Time moved, and at last the joyful news of Mr. Lincoln's election was trumpeted throughout the South. I say joyful, because, to the Knights, it was the gladdest intelligence that could have been borne them. All the principal castles now put on their holiday garments, and men were heard in the streets to thank God that the hour for "*Southern deliverance had come.*" (They should have thanked the devil, because he is their master.) Calhoun Castle, located at Charleston, considered itself as second to no place but Heaven, and hardly to that; and well might she have felt proud, because she was the mother of Southern harlots, and to her continuous and industrious workings, for many long years, were to be attributed the mighty growth of the secession snake, which, when she first found it, was indeed a very young one. No sooner had the news of the election of Lincoln been received, than every Knight in Charleston mounted a cockade on his hat, and ran through the streets, shouting, "GLORY! we are free! we are independent! The d—d old Union is gone to hell!"

Public meetings were called, and the greatest demonstrations were made. Everything was to be done in hot haste. All the speeches that were delivered at this period by the Knights partook of the hot, precipitous character of the conspirators. Notwithstanding their efforts to increase their numbers previous to the election, they were still in the minority, even in the Gulf States, and it was considered as fatal in the extreme to allow the common people of the country the least opportunity for thought or reflection. Many of these latter seemed to think that the matter of secession should be left with the border Slave States, it being clear to them that, inasmuch as these states were more interested than theirs, they should be allowed a controlling voice. Persons of this order of thinking termed themselves "Co-operationists," and favored the calling of a convention of all the Slave States. Hon. A. H. Stephens, of Georgia, was their leader; and had it not been for his great popularity, the co-operative theory would have dwindled much sooner than it did. It is, however, wonderful how the "Co-operationists," with a clear majority in every state but South Carolina, should have suffered themselves to be driven into the whirlpool of secession by the brow-beating force of the appellations "Submissionist," "Abolitionist."

It had never been the policy of the Knights to allow anything to be settled by the majority in a fair way. The cause which they advocated was not one which would admit of reflective deliberation, and hence, to allow the people time to reason in the premises, and determine the ultimate effects of secession upon the Slave States, or to ascertain the administrative policy of the newly elected President, would have proved fatal to their designs. It was a fact which none could deny, that the Democracy had a clear majority in both houses of Congress—a majority which could have held the administration in check, however much it might have been disposed to diverge from the path of constitutional rectitude—a majority which might have literally tied the President hand and foot, and have rendered him as incapable of encroaching upon "Southern rights" as an oyster is of making an aërial voyage across the Atlantic, or a Knight of getting to heaven—a majority even of Breckinridge Democrats, who would rather have their right arms torn from their sockets than deny that the extension of Slavery and the protection of the "nigger" is the genius of our Constitution and the sole end of Christianity—men whose motto was "*nigger first! country second!*" I say, all this was well known to the intelligent men of the nation, and yet the Southern people were constantly told that nothing but secession could save them from a subjugation too horrible even to contemplate. All the newspapers under the control of the K. G. C., were constantly teeming with editorials and contributions deeply deploring the humiliating fact that there were "yet a few" men in the South, "so unpatriotic to their states, and so untrue to themselves," as to oppose a declaration of "Southern independence." Secession orators, upon the stump, branded every man of the slightest Union tendency as a "cowardly truckler" and a "traitor to the South." Everything must be done *immediately;* it was worse than folly to await an overt act; Lincoln's election was, of itself, an overt act— no time was to be lost.

A weak cause always demands precipitancy. Of this the Knights were fully aware, and, therefore, took the advantage of the chagrined condition of the Southern people to "rush matters." Complete arrangements for the whole secession movement had been made long before the Presidential election, and, therefore, nothing remained but to carry it forward. No respect was to be shown the Government or the U. S. laws after Lincoln's ascension to the executive chair. Ample provisions were made for stealing on a large scale; United States senators and congressmen were to proceed to Washington and receive their regular pay for black-guarding the North, defaming the Government, and talking treason, and then, so soon as their states had seceded, whip off home like a thieving hound leaves a meat-house, with a ham in his mouth and his tail between his legs. All the plans for robbing the na-tional treasury, securing U. S. arms, etc., were also being put into execution, and the people know the result. They do n't, however, know all of them—that secession, with all its hellish concomitants was the legitimate result of the workings of a long and well or-ganized band of ROBBERS, more damnable than any who ever stood on the footstool, and PIRATES blacker than any who have preceded them to hell. Nor do they all know that some of the leading spirits of this clique had been at the very head of the American government for four years and more. There are, even yet, people who do not like to acknowledge that such men as Cobb and Floyd had been plotting the destruction of the American government, and the robbing of its treasury for nearly the whole time they were in its employ.

Finally, by the incessant hurrying and driving of the Knights. South Carolina was precipitated out of the Union, and her "in-dependence" declared. This they considered "knocking the key-stone out," which would be followed by the tumbling of the whole arch, as indicated by the motto inscribed upon some of the Charles-ton banners: "SOUTH CAROLINA LEADS, OTHERS WILL FOLLOW" No advantage was to be lost, and the old adage: "Give the devil an inch and he will take a foot," proved itself true in this instance. No sooner had the news of South Carolina's secession reached the principal cities in the Gulf States, than exciting bulletins were thrown broadcast, cannons fired, public mass meetings called, ex-citing speeches made, resolutions drawn up, read, and "adopted" by the crowd, and every other means of "firing the Southern heart" applied with great force. At all these meetings and demon-strations, special arrangements had been previously made by the

K. G. C. for the adoption of the resolutions they intended presenting. Thus, it was generally arranged that a certain number of the "chivalry" should, after taking a sufficient quantity of the inspiring beverage, go into the assembly where the meeting was to be held, "hurra for South Carolina" and "the South," and curse Lincoln, the Union, and every man that would submit to "Abolition rule." Of course, respectable gentlemen knew not how to successfully withstand this kind of brutal persuasion. I do not know whether this could be called "coercion" or not; but I can certainly see very little difference between whisky and mob suasion, and what some people call coercion. Perhaps the question might be settled by Webster, were it not that, in these latter days, that inferior lexicographer had been superseded by such learned dignitaries as Vallandigham and Gen. Joe Lane. Now, about this time, it was ascertained that the people in the North were getting *exceedingly* anxious about the Union. The telegraph was repeatedly announcing the calling and holding of "big mass meetings," the passage of "conciliatory resolutions," etc. These were laughed to scorn, derided, scoffed. One artistic Knight, who was a native of Boston, Mass., even went so far as to produce a couple of pictures expressive of the extreme plasticity of the Philadelphians. The first of these pictures presented a view of the citizens of the City of Brotherly Love, immediately after the election of Lincoln, paying homage to "Old Abe," and a big "nigger" who stood by his side as Mr. Hamlin. The second presented the same citizens after the secession of South Carolina, driving the "nigger," with clubs and hounds, back to that state, and kicking "Honest Old Abe" off a rickety old bench, which bore the inscription "Chicago Platform" unto another called "Compromise." These pictures were reproduced in great numbers, and sent, per mail, to every castle in the country. They were also sent to certain private individuals in some of the Northern Border State towns. I was informed that no less than fifty were mailed to northern Knights. The offers of compromise, and the repeal of Personal Liberty Bills by the North were considered not only humiliating to those who offered them, but insulting to those to whom they were offered. By some they were presumed to be hypocritical artifices, intended to hold the South in the Union while she should be lashed by slavery restriction. The truth is, the K. G. C. would accept no compromise, and none could have been framed to suit them. Secession they had been working zealously to achieve for several years, and secession they were bound to have. They had expended time and money; they had sacrificed the last vestige of honor, and gone, heart and soul, into the most diabolical plots and conspiracies for secession, and no compromise short of the adoption, by the North, of the proposed Confederate constitution, would have satisfied them.

In the mean time, there was immense excitement in Congress, as everybody knows. All sorts of modes of adjustment were being proposed there; almost every man seemed to have his own way of "saving the Union." Knights heeded none, cared for none. But among all others, the vigorous plan proposed by such men as Wade, of Ohio, and Andy Johnson, of Tennessee, produced the most decided effect. The only practical mode of affecting Secessionists is to make them either angry or afraid. The speeches of Johnson did both—angry, because he was decidedly hostile to their plans, whereas being a Southron, they thought he should be their friend—afraid, because, in consequence of his great popularity in Tennessee, they had good reason to believe he might prove a serious drawback to them in that state. If every Senator and Congressman who had taken the solemn oath to obey and defend the United States Constitution had been as faithful to his pledge as Johnson was, the Confederates would never have gained the time on the government they did. But with a weak-spined. indecisive, disconcerted, treacherous Congress, a majority of genuine Knights in the Cabinet, and a literal MUD MAN in the Presidential chair, they had ample time and facilities to drag six more states out of the Union. occupy forts, steal arms, fortify themselves, and laugh defiance in the very face of the government.

Among all the compromises proposed, that known as the Crittenden Compromise seemed to attract most attention. It will be remembered that Jeff Davis proposed that if the Republicans would present this compromise "in good faith," the South would be satisfied. Never did a greater lie escape from under the forgehammer of the father of lies than was this. In the first place, he (Davis) is one of the oldest Knights in the South, and had been the chief devil in all the black work described in the preceding pages, especially that of the three last years, to wit: 1858-'59-'60, and had sworn in castle to take the South out of the Union, if it were in his power to do so. In the second place, he had written all the principal castles to work steadily and earnestly: that the Knights in Congress and in the Cabinet were acting their parts nobly, (the parts they had to perform were blackguarding and stealing,) and that everything betokened the speedy achievement of Southern independence. In the third and last place, he knew that such a thing as the offering of the Crittenden Compromise "in good faith," by the Republicans, was an utter impossibility. Then, asks the reader, what was Davis's object in making the proposition? It was, that the eyes of the country might be blinded to the real character and objects of the Secessionists, and thereby an opportunity afforded for the more successful carrying out of their nefarious plans, in the first place; and, in the second place, that the people of the North might be led to believe that the Southern States would be satisfied with what was, by many, thought to be a fair compromise. The latter consideration was one of no small value, since it was presumed that the offers of "fair adjustment" by the South would go very far to strengthen and increase their friends, and disarm their foes in the North. During the early compromise discussions in Congress, many of the hotter Secessionists in the Gulf States were declaring they would have no compromise; but Jeff wrote them to be still and allow "things to work as long as they would work," as by that means "much valuable time was to be gained." The injunction was obeyed. Finally, a "Peace Conference" was called by the *commanding* voice of Virginia, and much "valuable time" was gained by its pointless, useless deliberations. It was about as well known before, as after, the meeting of the Peace Conference, that the North would never accept the proposed "ultimatum" of Virginia: because, in truth, the so-called ultimatum was nothing more nor less than the Breckinridge platform stewed down; and the men who drew it up, being mostly Knights, so far from wishing to settle the disturbances of the country by it, only aimed to carry out the deep laid plans of Davis, in allaying Northern suspicion, dividing Northern sentiment, and winning Northern sympathy, while their brothers in Washington were stealing, and those in the seceding states were robbing and preparing for defense.

·CHAPTER VI.

CORRESPONDENCE BETWEEN SOUTHERN AND NORTHERN KNIGHTS—
MEN AND MEANS PROFFERED—THE PLAN TO ASSASSINATE LINCOLN
AND SEIZE THE CAPITAL—LINCOLN'S INAUGURAL—THE "COERCION"
BUGBEAR OF THE K. G. C.—EXCITEMENT IN THE COTTON STATES—
THE MILITARY SPIRIT AROUSED—FLOYD'S TREASON—STATEMENT OF
THE "STEALINGS"—A REVIVAL OF THE UNION FEELING PRIOR TO
THE FALL OF SUMTER—THE "CONFEDERATE STATES'" GOVERN-
MENT—THE ATTACK ON SUMTER A SOUTHERN NECESSITY—THE
ORDER BECOMING UNPOPULAR, AND AN INCREASED MILITARY SPIRIT
NECESSARY TO REVIVE IT—THE BORDER STATES AND THE KNIGHTS
THEREOF—SPEECH OF A KENTUCKIAN—THE RATTLESNAKE'S CHARM
—THE LOVE FOR THE AMERICAN FLAG.

DURING the winter of 1860–'61, an extensive correspondence
was going on between Southern and Northern Knights, in which
the latter were representing the attachment to "Black Republicanism" as growing "small by degrees and beautifully less."
Some of these correspondents even went so far as to undertake
to prove that, in case of a revolt of the South, Mr. Lincoln, who
had not yet been inaugurated, could not raise half as many
men to fight for "the Union, the Constitution, and the enforcement of the laws," as could be sent South to assist in maintain-
ing "Southern rights." I did not have an opportunity to read or
copy any of the numerous letters written by the *Northern*
"chivalry," but was informed, by leading spirits of the Order, that
they had every assurance that they would obtain all the help in
the North they desired, both in the way of men and means. A
certain gentleman in Evansville, Ind., had promised a couple of
regiments, armed and equipped. A certain very prominent politician in Ohio had made a similar demonstration of his devotion
to the South. Another, of the latter stripe, in New York, had
promised a brigade of five thousand men, furnished for the war.
The above individuals were to procure their arms, etc., from the
United States in the same manner as those of their Southern
brethren had taken them in their section.

The inauguration of Lincoln being near at hand, some of the
K. G. C. bethought themselves that it would be a very fine idea
to assassinate him, and capture Washington, inasmuch as such a
thrilling movement would strike terror to the hearts of the "Abolitionists," afford an opportunity to rob the National Treasury,
and thus secure the entire field in advance. I am ashamed to
own that there were not a few sneaking devils north of Mason

and Dixon's line who counseled this diabolical policy, and promised assistance in its prosecution. Now, had it not been for the encouragement given them from Northern quarters, the Southern Castles would never have matured the plan for the Capital's seizure as far as they did.

The plan alluded to, of which the people of the country generally had several hints, was as follows: About one thousand men, armed with bowie knives and pistols, were to meet secretly at Baltimore, where they were to secure the services of the Plug Uglies. Thence they were to proceed to Washington, on the day previous to the inauguration, and stop at the hotels as private citizens, after which their leader was to reconnoiter and select the most effective mode of operations on the succeeding day. This scheme was not encouraged by Jeff Davis, as he was not yet quite crazy enough to think that a few dozen of the "chivalry" could terrify the whole world by one demonstration. Wigfall, however, thought it a "capital" idea, in more senses than one, and urged its vigorous prosecution. Fortunately, the plot was discovered, to some extent, in time to give Gen. Scott an opportunity to present some very forcible, and, with the K. G. C., decisive arguments against it. I know the Governor of Maryland tried to make it appear that no contemplated plan for the assassination of the President elect existed; but he really knew about as little of the matter as Mr. Lincoln himself, and had he known it, would doubtless have done all in his power to conceal the matter, when he saw the preparations being made to prevent it, in order to preserve the *fair fame of Baltimore*. Finally, the day for the inauguration (March 4, 1861) arrived, and the presence of Scott's U. S. troops, and the grim appearance of his flying artillery, made the occasion as peaceful as it was imposing The anxiously looked for inaugural address was delivered, and sent forth on the wings of the telegraph to all parts of the country. In the South it was received as a "coercive" document, while in the North, the majority regarded it as a conservative exposition of policy. Even the majority of Northern Democrats with whom I had an opportunity of conversing, thought the President could have said no less than he did, and abide by the Constitution. The mere intimation contained in the inaugural speech that the laws would be enforced, was all the Knights desired. This was "coercion" enough for them, and, in their estimation, no epithet was too contemptible to apply to those who indorsed it, whether living North or South. Here was another chance to sweep loyal Southern men from their position of honor into the secession hell.

After Mr. Lincoln's inauguration, one of the first questions for him to settle was, " What shall we do with the Confederates and the forts?" A question more difficult of solution never came before an administration. Mr. Floyd, Buchanan's Secretary of War, had

devoted about one out of the four years of the preceding administration to the removal of arms in large quantities from the Northern
and Border Slave States to the six Cotton States, while Toucey, the
then Secretary of the Navy, had sent the large majority of our
available ships-of-war to distant foreign stations—so far off, in fact,
that they have not, even at the date I am now writing, returned;
Charleston rebels had garrisoned Fort Moultrie, and erected the
most powerful and effective batteries all around Sumter, supported
by a force of seven thousand men; in all the seven seceded states
men by thousands were being mustered into the "Confederate"
service, drilled and equipped for war; and, more deplorable than
all else, there were scores of men in the loyal states who declared
they could not support Mr. Lincoln in a "coercive" policy. In
short, the new Administration was literally tied hand and foot,
and the most that it could do was to await the course of events,
and take opportunity by the forelock.

Lest *some* persons should doubt the truth of the allegations I
have made against Floyd, I have thought it well to present the
proofs. The following is from the Richmond *Examiner,* a Southern paper, especially devoted to the cause of secession:

"The facts we are about to state are official and indisputable.
Under a single order of the late Secretary of War, the Hon. Mr.
Floyd, made during last year, (1860,) there were one hundred
and fifteen thousand improved muskets and rifles transferred from
the Springfield armory and Watervliet arsenal to different arsenals
in the South. The precise destination that was reached by all
these arms, we have official authority for stating to have been as
follows:

	Percussion Muskets.	Altered Muskets.	Percussion Rifles.
Charleston (S. C.) Arsenal	9,280	5,720	2,000
North Carolina Arsenal	15,408	9,520	2,000
Augusta (Ga.) Arsenal	12,380	7,620	2,000
Mount Vernon, Alabama	9,280	5,720	2,000
Baton Rouge, Louisiana	18,520	11,420	2,000

"The total number of improved arms thus supplied to five de-
positories in the South, by a single order of the late Secretary of
War, was 114,860. What numbers are supplied by other and
minor orders, and what number of improved arms had, before the
great order, been deposited in the South, can not now be ascertained."

Besides this, a Memphis paper gives the following list of "seiz-
ures" of Federal arms by the Confederates, other than those in
Floyd's list:

Baton Rouge... 70,000
Alabama Arsenal... 28,000
Elizabeth, North Carolina................................... 30,000
Fayetteville, North Carolina................................ 35,000
Charleston 23,000
Norfolk 7,000

Total...193,000

Thus it appears that nearly three hundred thousand of the best arms of the Federal Government were put within the reach of its sworn enemies long before the election of Abraham Lincoln to the Presidency; and yet there were men among us, pretending to be loyal, who, up to the very day of Sumter's bombardment, declared the "South only wanted her rights;" that she could be easily "compromised back into the Union;" and that it would be a fratricidal crime to "*coerce*" her. According to the advanced views of this progressive age, it is very wrong to "coerce" a regularly organized band of burglars and robbers to justice. I presume that if the devil was to lead his impish legions to the very portals of Paradise, and threaten to bombard the New Jerusalem, it would be very "*coercive*" in JEHOVAH to send Michael and his army to repulse him.

Time progressed, and it began to appear that Lincoln's course was to be a peaceful one. This had the effect to induce the Union men of the South—for there were yet many there—to believe that, perhaps, a brighter day was ahead. In fact, the Union feeling was becoming so strong, from the lapse of excitement, that, toward the close of March, Union flags were raised in Mobile and Natchez. The Knights were not blind to this reaction. A little time and reflection, they knew, would ruin their enterprise. Meantime, many who had been "coerced" into castle were withdrawing, and it became clearly obvious that, without some new excitement, the cause of the devil would suffer a most inglorious defeat in Alabama, at least. The truth is, the people in nearly all the Cotton States were growing tired of so much extra taxation and slavish drudgery for the mere sake of sustaining the name of the "Southern Confederacy." As a means of keeping up "the interest," the Montgomery Congress appointed and sent commissioners to Washington to treat with the President, a good deal after the manner that his Satanic Majesty treated with Jesus Christ on the mount. If these commissioners were not officially received, it was to be taken for granted that Lincoln intended "coercion;" and yet no human being, with any knowledge of the Federal Constitution, could explain how the President could negotiate with the "Confederate Commissioners" without violating his oath. The Confederate Congress, which had met at Montgomery, framed a Constitution, elected a President, (Davis,) a Vice President, (Stephens,) and formed a provisional, or, more properly speaking, bogus government, could not confer the constitutional authority upon Lincoln to receive their bastard commissioners; Mr. Lincoln himself could not do it without having a new constitution forged for the occasion—which a good many Northerners seemed anxious he should do; so what, in the name of common sense, could be done to prevent that thing, so much dreaded by Northerners, and so terribly hated by Southrons, called "*coercion?*"

In the mean time, something was to be done with Forts Sumter and Pickens. If they were not evacuated, that was to be considered "coercion;" if they were to be reinforced, that was *awful* "coercion;" finally, if their starving garrisons were to be furnished something to eat, that was "*treacherous* coercion." In short, everything looking toward the retention of the Federal property was construed into "coercion." The "Confederate Commissioners" proposed to *purchase* the United States property within their boundary, in order to "save bloodshed." The leaders in the bogus government desired to create the impression that they intended to exhaust every peaceable method for securing the acknowledgment of their independence before resorting to arms, while, in reality, the uppermost desire in their piratical hearts was that they might have a battle; for, without a battle or two, there was not the least hope that the Border Slave States could be induced to secede. In proof of this assertion, I refer the reader to the historical fact that, when Mr. Lincoln had, through the advice of his military functionaries, concluded to evacuate Sumter, the authorities at Charleston refused to allow it on any other than their own conditions. They would agree to nothing but an unconditional surrender; would not allow that the fort should be claimed as United States property, nor that Major Anderson should even be allowed to salute his flag, on leaving it.

The ostensible objects, therefore, in sending the "Confederate Commissioners" to Washington were, in the first place, to procure a battle; in the second place, to avail themselves of sufficient time and sympathy to make ample preparations for the future; and, in the third place, by their hypocritical pretensions to a desire for peace, to inflame and draw off the Border Slave States.

Prominent members of the K. G. C. in the latter-named states had written to the authorities in Montgomery, informing them that the Order was becoming so unpopular in their region that, in many instances, castles were obliged to surrender their charters; that their neighbors were becoming even disgusted with the Provisional Government and the movements of the seceded states, and that without something to excite their *Southern pride*, the cause would be lost beyond redemption. A battle at Sumter or Pickens would excite that pride, and advantage must be taken of the first opportunity for a collision. I was in Kentucky about this time, (latter part of March, 1861,) and many of the best citizens of that state told me that they (the Kentuckians) had no sympathy with South Carolina, the leader of the rebellion; that they even hated her, but that, in case of a "coercive policy" on the part of the Federal Administration, *State pride* would carry them with her.

Southern pride is a thing of remarkable sensitiveness; so sensitive, in fact, that, when wounded, it induces men who pretend to be very intelligent to overlook all their political, social, and personal interests for the mere sake of resentment. I heard a man deliver a speech in Owensboro', Kentucky, in which he declared that secession was unconstitutional, and that every intelligent man knew there was no such thing as "the right of secession;" that, under existing circumstances, there was no excuse justifying the act; that the mere election of any man according to the prescribed mode of the Constitution, did not justify any state in leaving the Union; that Lincoln had done nothing to warrant such an action; that it was not probable he would; and that, in reality, every man who favored or advocated secession was, according to the laws of nations and according to the laws of the United States, a traitor and a rebel. "But," said he, "our interests, our sympathies are with the South, and we must go wherever she does. If we do not, we are lost, irrecoverably lost." He then referred to the fact that, during the late presidential canvass, he had labored zealously for the election of Bell and Everett; that he had always been a Union man, had ever loved the Union, and that no man had ever done more to prevent dissolution than he, as long as he thought it rational to indulge hope, but that the secession of South Carolina was, to him, the death-knell of the Union. Then, in the most touching and eloquent terms, he alluded to the old American flag; said that with his very mother's milk he had imbibed an indescribable love and reverence for that flag; that his grandfather had spent the vigor of his youth and the flower of his manhood in defending the banner of the free in '76; that his father, with his only uncle, (David Crockett,) had both fallen upon the battle-field, each fighting, as long as life and action remained, to sustain the honor of the glorious old stars and stripes; that no flag on earth could ever occupy the place in his affections that the old American ensign had. "But," said he, "I do not like the hands it has fallen into. I am a Southern man, we are all Southern men, and a Northern sectional candidate has been elected by a sectiona. vote. Our sister Southern States have become indignant at this action, and have seceded from the Union; and although we—many of us, at least—part with the old Union and the old flag with sighs and regrets, we are forced to do it, or submit ourselves to a tyrannical and oppressive 'Abolition' majority, where we will be worse than slaves. There would have been no necessity for this act of rebellion—for rebellion it is—if our sisters on the Gulf coast had staid in the Union, and thereby preserved a Democratic majority. So that it is not really any objection to the old Government, or hatred to Lincoln, that carries a great many of us with the seceding states, but a consciousness of our absolute inability to stand alone and single-handed against the North, who undoubtedly will, now that so many Southern States have gone, rule us with a rod of iron."

The foregoing is, substantially, a speech made in Owensboro', on the evening of March 28, 1861, by J. W. Crockett, of Kentucky. I have quoted it from memory. The best I could do, therefore, was to give the substance. The style of the speaker can never be conveyed to one that never heard him. J. W. Crockett is an orator of great force and surpassing eloquence, and I do not remember to have ever heard a speech that produced the effect on me that this one did. The speaker was naturally a noble man, of generous impulses and warm sympathies, of hopeful soul and patriotic heart, but in the worst company that could have been selected for him. As he spoke of the glory of the old flag and the love he bore it, tears gathered in his eyes and trickled down his cheeks, which were covered with the blush of shame; the expression of his large gray eye was that of mingled sorrow and regret, while his manly breast heaved tumultuously, almost to the choking of his utterance. In short, he seemed as "a strong man bound," without the power of escaping from those who were applying to him the excoriating lash of disunion, and forcing him to utter *their* sentiments, not his. He had been taught by his mother to love the country and the flag for which his father had died; he had been taught by her to respect the truth and acknowledge the superior claims of justice; he had been taught to avoid evil and keep out of the way of evil doers. But the insidious serpent of secession had coiled itself about his soul, fastened its poisonous fangs upon his heart, and destroyed his manhood.

Nor is he the only one who has been falsely lured from the path of loyalty into the disunion hell. Hundreds, if not thousands, of others are in the same deplorable condition. Who is silly enough to presume that men thus humbled by the remembrance of the past, men thus oppressed by the weight of a guilty conscience, can fight for what they know to be an unjust cause, as the soldier of freedom can battle for the Union, the Constitution, and the star-spangled banner? I am fully convinced that, before this war is ended, hundreds of Knights who have been "coerced" into castle and the advocacy of secession, will ask protection under the flag of the Union. Will not the response of every true American be, "They shall have it?"

But I am about to allow my feelings to carry me too far from the point. The object in quoting so largely from the speech of J. W. C—— was to show that the Southern people were growing absolutely tired of secession, and that some even of the K. G. C were beginning to reflect, and repent of their crimes. The Confederate leaders were not blind to these facts. Something, therefore, to frenzy their blood, and prevent them from returning to sanity, was indispensable to self-preservation. Meantime, South Carolinians were "spoiling for a fight." They had gone to too much expense and trouble not to have one. Mr. Lincoln having refused to sacrifice his own and the nation's honor on the altar of the "nigger baby," by not submitting to Jeff Davis's demand of an unconditional surrender of Forts Sumter and Pickens, it was considered that a fine opportunity for arousing the spirit and pride of the "chivalry" had arrived. It was now generally understood to be the policy of the Administration to retain the forts without reinforcements. But as the garrisons could not live without something to eat, and as their supplies were about exhausted, the reprovisioning of the forts was unavoidable. The attempt to carry food to Sumter by an unarmed vessel was the signal for its bombardment, April 12, 1861, which resulted in its final surrender. Meanwhile, it had been threatened that, at the shedding of the first blood, an army would immediately be ready to march on Washington; and numbers of weak-minded men in the Border States were saying that, although they had voted for Bell and Everett, and done all they could to prevent dissolution, yet, in case a fight occurred, they would be forced to go with the South.

Really, this thing called Southern sympathy is the most remarkable thing I have ever come in contact with. To illustrate: Some time before the battle at Fort Sumter, a secession flag was being raised in Mobile, around which were gathered several men who had, until the departure of their state from the Union, been warmly opposed to disunion. Among these was a man who, in all respects, bore the marks of a gentleman. When the flag was run up, and the crowd were cheering it lustily, this man, to be in the fashion, took off his hat, waved it three times round his head without saying a word; and just as he was replacing it, turned from the intent gaze of a bitter secessionist who stood at his elbow, and drawing a long sigh, remarked, in a suppressed tone, to himself: "*But that is not the star-spangled banner. It will never be the flag of* AMERICA; *and who can hope for the protection under it we enjoyed under the stars and stripes?*" Another instance: I was in Kentucky immediately after the Sumter engagement, and the Knights in the town I was stopping at having thoroughly "fired the Southern heart," and forced nearly every man either into their own way of thinking or to utter silence, were, on the 15th of April, engaged in hoisting a J. D. flag, with fifteen stars instead of seven. In the assembly gathered for this treasonable purpose was a gray-haired veteran of ninety-six years, who had served through the war of 1812, and had also fought in the frontier wars; was a colonel under Harrison, and was in the battle of Tippecanoe. When the emblem of rebellion had been thrown to the breeze, and the half-drunken crowd were expressing their approbation in demoniac yells, the old soldier, for the first time in several years, raised himself erect, and, with tears in his eyes, remarked: "*I am as good a Southern Rights man as anybody, but I can never recognize that flag. I could fight the Yankees or the devil under the stars and stripes, but under no other ensign.*"

Thus it is with thousands who will compose the rebel army. The infatuation which induces the belief that they are to fight in defense of their "homes," "rights," and "*sacred soil*," which are being invaded by a ruthless foe, is nothing to compare with the patriotic love and veneration for the stars and stripes which pervades the entire body of our soldiery. And this feeling has not altogether died out with those who will fight against that flag, under such misguided leaders as Jeff Davis and Beauregard. The Southern people have, in every war in which we have hitherto been engaged, displayed great courage and gallantry; but I firmly believe that the demoralizing influence of the unholy cause in which they are now required to enlist, will render them totally incapable of retaining their former prestige

CHAPTER VII.

THE BOMBARDMENT OF FORT SUMTER—ITS EFFECT UPON THE BORDER STATES—AGENTS OF THE K. G. C. AT WORK—THEIR COOL RECEPTION IN SOUTHERN INDIANA AND ILLINOIS—GAG LAW AND MOB RULE—PRENTICE, GUTHRIE, JOHNSON, AND BROWNLOW CLASSED AS "HARD-SHELLS"—THE MANNER IN WHICH PROSELYTES ARE MADE—THE CANDIDATE IN THE ANTE-ROOM—THE "PRELIMINARY DEGREES," THEIR FORMS, SYMBOLS, AND OATHS—THE "OUTER TEMPLE"—ITS INITIATORY CEREMONIES—THE OUTSIDE DESIGNS OF THE ORDER—HOW CONVENTIONS, LEGISLATURES, AND ELECTIONS ARE CONTROLLED—"KNIGHTS' SAFETY GUARDS" AND "KNIGHTS GALLANT"—SOUTHERN LADIES SENT NORTH AS SPIES—PLANS TO DESTROY PROPERTY AT THE NORTH—NORTHERN SYMPATHIZERS.

THE battle at Fort Sumter had, to a considerable extent, the effect in the Border States that the secession leaders desired it should. Virginia was, by the villainous acts of the Knights, declared out of the Union, as was likewise Arkansas and Tennessee, and it was fully expected that every remaining Southern State would soon follow, for without all of them it was not hoped to make a successful attack on Washington. It was also confidently expected, from the representations of Northern men, that their section would be greatly divided in sentiment, and that much assistance might be looked for in that direction. It is not to be wondered at that they should have expected succor from the North, when, up to the very day of Lincoln's proclamation, such influential men as the Hon. Mr. B——, and H——, of Indiana, the Hon. Mr. V——, of Ohio, and other equally prominent men had promised that thousands of men in the North "would help the South, if the South would help herself." This latter quotation I take from the speech of an Indiana State Senator, made in Kentucky but a few days before the bombardment of Fort Sumter. Said Honorable has since renounced "the faith" and gone over to the side of the Union. Many others have "gone and done likewise." Hope their repentance is genuine, and that they will "bring forth fruits meet for repentance."

About this time, agents were sent into all the border Slave and *Free* States to stir up the Southern feeling, assist in the convocation of Secession Conventions, and do all they could in the promotion of that outside pressure which is indispensable to secession everywhere. The first thing for these agents to do, was to institute castles wherever a sufficient number of the friends of "Southern Rights" could be called together for the purpose. Those delegated to Tennessee, Missouri, Arkansas, Virginia, etc., reported favorably; but those who visited Southern Indiana and other Northern border States, found the soil and climate very unfavorable, not only to the growth of secession sprouts, but to their own personal comfort. To their great mortification, they saw that no man north of the Ohio river was willing to tie the portion of the state in which he lived to the tail end of the rattlesnake, or fight under the flag of three stripes and seven stars. Whenever one of these Southern agents came in contact with a native Northern Knight, he was immediately advised that the "Abolitionists" had the whole North, and that it was even inimical to one's individual well-being to say anything *indicating* sympathy with Jeff Davis. The result was that they left in great disgust. Meanwhile, the Northern Secessionists found the Union, or, as they term it, "Abolition" feeling, growing so strong that they were denied the "*liberty of speech,*" and were forced to content themselves with stretching their countenances, drawing long sighs, and *deploring "the condition of the country."*

The knowledge of the fact that the whole North, with its superior population and wealth, was a unit in defense of the Union; that Southern Indiana and Illinois would not "*secede*" and go with the rattlesnake government; that not a corporal's guard of men could be found in any Northern State who would fight under any other than the old flag; that many hitherto staunch Knights in the North were withdrawing from their castles, some of them even enlisting in the United States service, and that, consequently, they had been most grossly deceived respecting the status of Northern affairs—I say, a consciousness of these facts did more to retard the progress of rebellion than anything else for the time. A vigorous attempt would have been immediately made after the battle at Sumter to capture the United States' Capital but for the said reverse the cause of disunion had met with in the great North. But the chagrin experienced in consequence of their unexpected disappointment in the Free States, only nerved the K. G. C. to more powerful efforts in the South. Castles were built up at every little town and cross-roads where one dozen of the faithful could be mustered. In every locality where they had the majority, and even in some instances where they were in the minority, the gag-law was brutishly enforced by mob suasion. Wherever they had the power to carry forward their designs in the Border Slave States, they were to denounce, in the bitterest terms, every man who would not work in concert with them. Men, whether natives of North or South, who opposed them, were to be dealt with as traitors. I saw a man ordered to leave a little town on the Kentucky shore, in half an hour's time, or remain and be hung, although he had been born and reared in the place. In short, all the "coercive" appliances were to be used in Border States which had been so successful in the seceded States. But one very serious obstacle in the path of their progress was the strong and decided stand which some of the ablest and most influential of their own statesmen were taking in favor of the Union. Such men as Prentice, Harney, Guthrie, Dixon. Brownlow, Johnson, Nelson, and others of that class, stood greatly in their way. These were men to be feared far more than Northern foes, for their talents, and influence in the South, being commensurate with their patriotism, their blows at the snake of secession were powerful and effective. All hail to those patriotic giants who, even yet, with their love of country undimmed by the sulphurous smoke of the despotic hell by which they are surrounded on every hand, dare to unsheath their claymores and wield them in defense of that government to which they have ever stood devoted. In order to the rapid propulsion of the secession car, such men as the afore-mentioned were either to be persuaded off the track, or run over. In other words, if it was found impossible to win them over to secession, they were to be made way with. In castle numerous plans were proposed to effect these designs. Brownlow and John-son they did not hope to convert to their faith; consequently they were to have their "lights put out." But it was thought that pos-sibly, by getting up a strong outside pressure, such as Prentice and Guthrie might be induced to recant. In fact, there were scores of Knights who, notwithstanding their new-born zeal in the cause of the devil, still loved Prentice. He had been their great guide when they were old Whigs; he had, for many years, led them in his own channel of political philosophy; he had, from their earliest recollections, invigorated them with his wit and inspired them with his poetry. In short, he had been the monarch of their souls, the idol of their affections; and it was no ordinary punish-ment to them to be forced to part with him now. They were, therefore, willing to extend to him more than ordinary lenity, sincerely hoping that in time he would see the "error of his ways," and repent in "sack cloth and ashes." They also pre-sumed that Prentice, once fairly on the side of disunion, and Kentucky was out in a hurry. But for others, for whom they lacked the affection they bore Prentice, and who, they apprehended, could never, by any influence, be induced to desert the old ship, they had in store a *vigorous* treatment. Various plans were pro-posed in castle to get what were termed the hard-shells out of the way. Some of them were to be insulted, and, by that means, drawn into a fight, which was to terminate in their murder. Others were to be poisoned, or assassinated. No act was to be considered criminal which had for its object the destruction of "Abolition-ists." I heard one man say in Kentucky, that he could cut Arch Dixon's throat with more pleasure than he could eat his dinner when hungry. At the time I left the latter-named state, I fully expected, from what I had seen and heard in castle and out, that several of her best statesmen would have been foully dealt with ere this. They were, however, put on their guard, to my knowledge, and that, together with the great reaction which has taken place in many parts of Kentucky, has, doubtless, prevented the commission of some of the blackest crimes ever recorded.

The extent to which dark and villainous intriguery is being practiced by the Knights of the Golden Circle, or, as they should be termed, *The Imps of Hell*, at this time, has rarely ever been equaled in the annals of highway robbery. The very manner in which they make proselytes is in itself more damnable than any-thing which even that old serpent, the devil, has ever invented. For instance, a man comes into town from the farming districts. He is immediately beset on all sides, and questioned respecting his politics, etc., in the following manner: "Sir, are you a Southern Rights' man?" "Well, yes, I believe I go in for the rights of the South." "Well, there are one or two gentlemen up here at the corner, Mr. —— and Dr. ——, who desire to see you a few minutes. Will you be kind enough to go with us?" "Certainly." They proceed to the "corner" spoken of, when the "gentlemen" alluded to come forward, take the farmer by the hand, greeting him very warmly, and ask him if he would not like to co-operate with them in a plan to defend the "homes and firesides" of himself and neighbors against "Yankee invasion." "Why, are they going to invade *us*?" "Yes, *certainly*. We have it, upon reliable authority, that several hundred of the d——d Hoosiers are within a few hours' march of this place." By this time the old man's eyes begin to stand out so plumply from their orbits, that in passing *too* near a brush fence there would be danger of him losing them; and with his jugulars protruding like ropes from either side of his neck, and his mouth thrown wide open, he fairly belches out the indignant interrogatory: "WHAT HOOSIERS?" "Why, some of those Abolition Hoosiers from Pike, and Posey, and Gibson counties, with a large number from the Yankee portion of the state up about the lakes. You know those Abolitionists in Pike, who have always been in the habit of hiding our *niggers* when they ran up about Petersburg, don't you?" "Ye-es, I have often heard of them." "Well, they are at the head of the gang." "Well, I want it distinctly understood that I am in *all over* for any plan intended to check or punish *them*." The old gentleman is now asked to take a glass of Bourbon—a request with which every Kentuckian willingly complies—and go "up stairs" with them. On arriving "up stairs" he meets several, perhaps a couple of dozen, of the "chivalry," by whom he is surrounded and warmly welcomed. He is now led into an ante-room and requested to be seated until castle is opened. Castle being opened, fifteen—if they have that number present—of the Knights proceed to the ante-room, form a crescent-shaped circle, from the center of which the captain and lieutenant step forward a little in front, when the old gentleman is led by the conductor in front, facing the aforementioned officers, and asked, by the chief Knight; if "he has any objection to entering an Order

(47)

which, while it will not interfere with his *religious sentiments* nor political views, has for its main object the maintenance of Southern rights and the protection of Southern homes." He replies in the negative. He is then asked if he is willing to bind himself in an oath to aid and assist them in the furtherance of these objects. He answers in the affirmative. He has now passed what is termed the first of the "preliminary degrees," and is welcomed to the circle by a general shake-hands. The officers and the circle retire, while some one of the faithful remains outside to talk to him of the grandeur, the beauties, and the sublime and holy objects of the Order. Presently a rap is heard at the door of the ante-chamber, and the question is asked by the guard: "Who comes?" To which the lieutenant replies: "The friends of Southern rights, to welcome a brother." The door is then opened, and the circle again appears, the lieutenant bearing in his left hand a large crescent with fifteen stars set in its sides. Old gentleman is again brought up facing the captain and lieutenant, who are stationed in the front of the circle as before. The chief now enters into a somewhat elaborate explanation of the reasons why they conduct the proceedings of the Order in a secret manner; among other things, telling the candidate that such a manner of proceeding is necessary to concert and unity, which are the two first indispensables to success; and also that such a course is calculated to promote a fraternal and brotherly feeling among them; that the experience of the world has taught us that secret organizations are far more effective than public ones, the prejudice of many good people to the contrary notwithstanding.

These explanations having been made, candidate is asked if he is now willing to take an oath that he will never reveal anything he may see or hear during his initiation. He replies in the affirmative. The oath is now administered; and being further sworn to stand devoted to the cause and fortune of the South, he is considered through the second of the "preliminary" degrees. Circle with officers retire, the requisite preparations are made in the arrangement of symbols, etc., and castle is ready to receive candidate into the hall. At the proper signal he is led by conductor from the ante-chamber into castle, where he is again met by the circle, as in the last-named instance. Candidate is now to swear, in the presence of "God and these witnesses," (*it should be in the presence of the devil and his imps,*) that he " will aid and assist, to the extent of his ability, in promoting a permanent separation of all the Southern from the Northern States," and that he will, " both individually, and in concert with the brethren composing this Order, use his utmost efforts to ferret out, punish, and expel from Southern borders, all who, either directly or indirectly, favor the enemies of Southern rights." Having given his assent to this, he is considered through the third and last of the "preliminary" degrees. Candidate is again conducted to ante-chamber, when castle makes full preparations for receiving him into Outer Temple. These having been effected, initiate is again led into the hall, and received into the embrace of the circle as before. Circle now incloses him by forming a complete ring, when the chief announces to him, in the most solemn and dignified manner, that " he is now a KNIGHT OF THE GOLDEN CIRCLE." This is positively the first time he hears his name, and, in some instances, it makes him, as the Hoosiers say, " look wild." He is now sworn to regard his duty to his state and his state authorities, and his home and domestic interests as " paramount to his duty to the United States Constitution and all other human enactments." The pass-word, which is changed every three months, or oftener, if it is necessary to prevent impositions, is then given him, together with the signs of the Order, and he is, in all respects, a member of the Outer Temple of the ———— Castle of the Knights of the Golden Circle.

It will be observed that some insignificant changes have been made in the ritual within the last few months, by comparing the foregoing initiation with what has been said, in previous pages, of the form of receiving members one year or less ago. Just here I will remark that with the K. G. C. the ritual is by no means as permanent or unalterable as that of most other secret orders; and, in fact, nearly every castle is in the habit of modifying this instrument to suit the "peculiar" demands of the immediate locality in which it is intended to be used. For instance, in Kentucky and other Border States, in latter days, the various initiatory steps to the Inner Temple are much more gradual and conservative than they are in the Cotton States; and, in many cases, where it is known that the candidate is a more than usually moral man, and somewhat sensitive respecting oaths, the chief has the privilege of laying aside the ritual for the most part, and tolling the applicant in on his own hook. But the supposed case just cited unfolds the general plan, and it will be seen that the most flagrant misrepresentations, and the most unscrupulous lying are resorted to for the purpose of making additions. An honestly disposed man is picked up in the street, and is hardly aware of it before he has taken the most binding oaths to violate the constitution of his country, trample the United States laws under his feet, and assist, with his whole power, in the carrying out of the most treasonable and diabolical crimes against the government and its supporters. But so far as the government and formal regulations of the castles are concerned, they are of very little importance within themselves. It is the outside designs of the Order at this time, and the various plans adopted, from time to time, to prosecute them, that should receive most attention, inasmuch as they threaten not only the subsequent ruin and destruction of the American Republic, but menace the happiness and well-being of every neighborhood and family north of Mason and Dixon's line, especially those of the western Border States.

I will now proceed to give a systematic exposition of these designs, and their modes of prosecution, as far as I was able to obtain a direct knowledge of them up to the time I left the South, immediately after the fall of Sumter. In the first place, in order to drag the Border Slave States out of the Union, it is determined upon to either "coerce" the State Legislatures into the calling of conventions for the passage of secession ordinances, or call one themselves, through the Governor or otherwise. In the second place, in the election of delegates to such conventions they are bound to have their own kind of men chosen by the use of the following appliances: *First*, Large numbers of Knights from adjoining states are to be imported, armed, and prepared for any emergency. These are to attend the elections, and, if they can not succeed in casting their own illegal votes, are to stand around the polls, and by curses, threats, and even violence, if necessary, force weak-spined Union men to vote the Secession ticket. *Second*, Knights of the Inner Temple are, if possible, to be chosen as tellers and clerks of the various precincts at the day of election. *Third.* Between the time of the announcement and the holding of said election, all, or at least as many as possible, of those who are known to be staunch, immovable Union men, are to be driven out of their state, detained from the election, either by stratagem or force, or made way with. Nothing but the overawing influence of vastly superior numbers of resolute Union men, or the presence of United States soldiery, can prevent the carrying out of this part of the programme. After the submission of the ordinance to the popular vote by the convention, the same means are to be used in furtherance of its adoption as those applied in the previous election.

In the second place, after they have succeeded in getting out of the Union, they intend having committees, to be called "Knights' Safety Guards," appointed, to watch every man of whom they have the least doubt, and whether native of North or South, if any hold can be gained upon him, he is to be dealt with in any way the "Guards" may see proper. They need not bring such person before the proper authorities for a formal trial, but may barrel him up and throw him into a river, tar and feather him, and send him North, shoot, hang, or deal with him otherwise, as their "judgments" may dictate. Thirdly, guerrilla parties are to be formed, both to harrass Northern troops on their passage through their sections, and to make devastating forays upon the North. These are called, in castle, "KNIGHTS GALLANT." Their mission is wherever they wish to go, and their license to take what they can, and do what they please, except to injure or violate females or little children. "KNIGHTS GALLANT" are sworn to protect female virtue and children's lives, even at the peril of their own. By the "KNIGHTS GALLANT" provisions are to be secured from Northwestern States, in case of a scarcity in the South, for the Southern army. All the property or money they can obtain in the course of their perambulations is to be considered as *Southern wealth.* When Southern armies desire to march Northward, the services of the K. G. are to be secured as guides and scouts. A continual correspondence is to be kept up with the known and tried Knights of the North, so as to assist the K. G., either in making forays or conducting forces; to secure such knowledge of those points where provisions, stores, prizes, etc., may be taken with most ease, as was necessary, and also to ascertain by what routes such provisions and stores can be most easily conveyed to Southern borders. Fourthly, the true and faithful members of the Order living in the Northern States are to play the hypocrite on a most extensive scale, by making loud and enthusiastic professions of loyalty to the government, while, in the mean time, they are to act as spies, communicating to the nearest castles the various movements of Northern troops, and the most accessible routes of march and points of attack for Southern forces. Fifthly, influential members in the North are to be induced, if possible, to raise companies of militia under the requisition of President Lincoln, secure their arms and equipments, and then turn them over to the "Confederate" service; such companies being composed of men who are known to be true friends of the South. Just here I will drop a hint to the friends of American freedom. *No man in the North who expressed sympathy with the South, or who violently opposed the movements of the Government, until the overwhelming force of public opinion drove him into the Union ranks, should be trusted with any patriotic duty, or allowed to command even a corporal's guard of men, until he has furnished the most reliable evidence of loyalty; and, in many instances, where there is good reason to presume, from a man's past acts, that his feelings are strongly Southern, or that he is not fully trustworthy, even though from the first that he heard of the President's Proclamation calling for troops he has made strong Union professions, it is highly important to keep a close watch over him, and see that he gains no advantage.* I have, as yet, heard of but one place in any Northern state where any portion of that part of the Knights' programme under head fifth has been commenced, and that was in Martin County, Indiana. The man who was at the head of the movement is named Drongoole. (The Cincinnati papers call him, improperly, *Dromgoole.*) This imp, whom the devil will, doubtless, be ashamed to own, but who, in all probability, will soon resemble the famous violinist, Paginini, in one respect, viz.: his capacity to play on "*one string,*" wrote to the Corresponding Secretary of the Nashville Castle, where he holds his membership, informing said secretary, that he could easily raise a regiment of one thousand men in Martin County to fight for the South. The secretary replied, advising him to immediately communicate the glad tidings to Jeff Davis, as the case would be readily attended to. Drongoole did write Jeff, giving him the "*most satisfactory*" evidences of his ability to muster the aforementioned regiment into the "Confederate service." Jeff replied, commending his "true and faithful" servant very highly for his "noble and patriotic" endeavors; but, for one time in his life, at least, seemed to have been remiss in the exercise of those "*far-seeing*" qualities for which his confederates give him so much credit, in inclosing his letter in an envelope bearing the Confederate flag on its exterior.

The recognition of this emblem by the postmaster at Dover Hill resulted in the opening and reading of Jeff's epistle, the contents of which soon becoming public, so highly excited the "Confederate" patriotism of the citizens of Martin county, that they could not refrain from manifesting their otherwise inexpressible approbation of the noble Drongoole and his course, by means of fervent, patriotic kicks and blows, so well laid on that he came near yielding up the ghost. Drongoole, whether from the advice of his physician or not, concluded that it would be well for him to travel South a little for his health, before undertaking to lead a regiment of Martin county Hoosiers against "Lincoln's army."

But if he had not been detected in good time he would have effected much harm. There are others, who are far less suspected than he was, of whom we may expect more real harm. While passing through Sullivan county, on my way to Indianapolis, a certain gentleman residing in that county, told me, privately, that he intended raising a company of one hundred men to fight for Jeff Davis; at least he would make the attempt. He also told me that if Davis was to march an army through his neighborhood on that very day, devastating the country as he went, that he, with many more, would join him. This gentleman was not a member of the K. G. C., but had been under the special influence and teachings of one who lived in his immediate neighborhood; he had not yet caught the signal of silence, and was, therefore, openly expressing his imbibed sentiments. I talked with him shortly afterward, and he had, to all appearance, undergone a most wonderful and miraculous conversion. He was now a strong Union man, and a bitter enemy to Jeff Davis. This apparently remarkable change I could easily account for, when I had seen him, in the interim between the first and last conversations, talking with a certain individual who recognized the sign of the crescent. By some close maneuverings, I found that the last-mentioned individual had several proseltyes in and around his neighborhood, and that it was the intention of these to form a "*Home Guard*," to act in "*emergencies.*" They could not, however, be induced, by a certain gentleman who was then enrolling a company for Government service, to go *from* home to fight the battles of the country, although several of them were stout young men, foot-loose, and unemployed.

Mysteries of this kind require some explanation, and wherever they appear, should undergo the closest scrutiny. A close discerner of men and things can generally detect treachery, where it exists, in a man's motions and the expressions of his eye, whatever his lip pretensions may be; and in times such as these it is well, yea, even highly important, to exercise a most vigilant watch over all a man's little actions, where there is any just foundation for doubt.

But to the sixth plan in the secession programme of to-day.* This plan is to be carried out by sending such of the patriotic Confederate ladies as will come, into the Northern States, for the purpose of acting as corresponding agents and spies. While making pretensions that they are Southern refugees, and that they have been scared away from their homes by fears of negro insurrections, or that they are come North to improve their health and enjoy tranquillity of mind, they are to be constantly on the alert for news respecting the designs of the Government or the movements of armies, and transmit the same to the proper authorities in the South. Further, they are to act, wherever it is possible to do so, in the capacity of beasts of burden, (I do not use this term disparagingly,) to convey contrabrand articles to such agents or places as shall insure their safe delivery to the secessionists. This may seem highly improbable to many, but it should be remembered by all that a woman is decidedly a *great institution*, and that by means of such efficient and extensive modern facilities as crinoline, etc., she could effect considerable in the way of exporting small arms, percussion caps, etc.

In the present troubled condition of the country, the good citizens of the loyal states will experience no little difficulty in determining who is a spy and who is not, especially in the case of ladies; because there will be many fleeing to the North as real refugees; many who, in consequence of the miserable days and fearful, sleepless nights they have spent during long and gloomy weeks, will sacrifice home, with all its former endearments, for the sake of finding a place where they may rest their wearied frames and compose their excited minds. But while it is true that many truly noble and excellent women will seek the North for these purposes, and these alone, it is also true that some, at least, will come for far different purposes. It will, therefore, be necessary to be hospitable, while we are prudent; kind and sympathetic, while we are vigilant and watchful.

Finally, it is the intention of the K. G. C. to send incendiary agents—men who scruple at nothing, care for nothing—for the purpose of committing raids, destroying property, etc., wherever such service can in any way facilitate the cause of secession. For instance: When an army, or any considerable number of troops, are rendezvousing at a determinate point on the border,

* April 20, 1861.

and it is necessary, in order to the successful prosecution of any Confederate design, to have them removed, these incendiary agents are to set fire to some town or city near by, in order that the Government forces may be attracted from their post. Thus it was planned to burn New York, Boston, Philadelphia, and Cincinnati, just after the battle at Fort Sumter, to the end that the United States troops might be called away from Washington, and its capture thereby rendered easy. None but Knights of the Inner Temple are intrusted with this kind of work. They must be, at the same time, shrewd, active, bold, and faithful. Wonderful to say, some of the very agents who were to burn the cities just referred to, were not only residents of the places they intended to burn, but actually owned property in them. This, however, was to be "*indemnified*" by the Cotton Confederacy.

Nothing but the unanimous uprising of the loyal masses of the North, the exercise of an unexpected vigilance, and an unceasing watch-care, saved those cities. The great trouble here, as in the case of the female spies, is to know whom to watch, inasmuch as all of them make loud professions of loyalty so soon as they set foot on Northern soil. *The true policy is to watch everybody with whom we are unacquainted, until we have the most satisfactory evidence that they are true.* In point of close scrutiny and vigilance, we of the North are far behind the Southern people. No sooner does a stranger arrive at any Southern town or depot, than he is beset on all sides by "Knights' Safety Guards," or, as they are called by the outsiders, Vigilance Committees, who proceed immediately to quiz him in the most abrupt and complicated manner. He is examined and cross-examined in various ways, until the "chivalry" are thoroughly satisfied; he must reply to their questions in the most direct and unequivocal manner; he is allowed no room for dodges or evasions, but must come right up to the mark; and even after he has answered all questions in the most explicit and satisfactory manner, is still an object of suspicion and scrutiny. We, on the other hand, are exceedingly mild in our demands, careless, indifferent, and lenient; take it for granted that a man is loyal merely because he says he is, and frequently allow him even to talk treason, thinking that it don't amount to much, inasmuch as the Union sentiment is "so strong." I have heard men say things in Terre Haute and Indianapolis, in public places, for which, if we were half so vigilant as the K. S. G. in the South, we would hang them to the nearest tree we could find. Now, I do not propose that we should adopt the brutal, merciless system of the Knights, but that, in view of the real demands of the country, and the safety of our neighborhoods, families, and persons, we should see to it, and see to it *well*, that no man, whether neighbor or stranger, has an opportunity to do or say any harm.

CHAPTER VIII.

THE NORTH TOO CONFIDENT—THE SOUTHERN STRENGTH UNDERRATED
—THE EXTENT OF THE BROTHERHOOD AT THE NORTH, AND IN THE
BORDER STATES—KENTUCKY'S NEUTRALITY—THE "STATE GUARD"
CONTROLLED BY THE K. G. C.—THE GOVERNOR OF KENTUCKY A
KNIGHT—THE WAR OF 1861—JUSTICE UNKNOWN TO THE TRAITOR
FRATERNITY—THE SWORD THE ONLY ARGUMENT THAT WILL EXACT
JUSTICE—VIGILANCE AT THE NORTH ESSENTIAL—THE FEELING AT
THE SOUTH SINCE THE WAR BEGAN—NEGRO INSURRECTIONS—BRU-
TALITY OF THE KNIGHTS—THEIR MODE OF CARRYING ON THE WAR—
WHAT THEY INTEND TO ACCOMPLISH.

I FIND, in passing through Northern towns and neighborhoods,
that the people are entirely too confident in the strong arm of the
government and their own superior wealth and numbers. They
do not appear disposed to make any deductions in favor of the
South, in view of its more extensive and complex strategic system;
and, in many instances, when I have told them of the many
destructive secret plans of the secessionists, they seemed loth to
believe the statement; it appeared to them impossible that the
Southern traitors should have become "so grossly depraved." It is
wonderful, indeed, that the same robbers who coolly pocketed
thousands of dollars of our money and appropriated it to the
rebellious government, and who stole nearly three thousand stand
of our arms, and sent our army and navy so far out of reach that
we could not avail ourselves of their services in time of danger,
should subsequently plot the destruction of our towns and cities,
and the confiscation and appropriation of our property. Whether
my exposition of the thieving, murderous, destructive schemes of
the Confederate rebels is believed or not, they will, before the lapse
of many months, become so fully manifest, that even the most in-
credulous will be forced to acknowledge that what I have said is
true. But I sincerely trust that the honest warnings of one who
has repeatedly risked his life to obtain an actual knowledge of the
treacherous designs of the avowed enemies to American freedom,
may not pass unheeded. I earnestly hope that those who have
the direction of affairs, as well as private individuals, will keep
constantly before their minds the following facts: *First.* That
the present deplorable condition of the country has been brought
about by the continuous workings of that same diabolical clique
who began a regular system of slave piracy thirty years ago.
Second. That the whole course of that clique, from the first period
of its history to the present day, has been one of unexampled

villany and enmity toward the Federal Government. *Third.* That in view of the fact that they have, from the beginning, been duly conscious of the unjustifiableness of their course, the treachery of their designs, and the deficiency of their resources, they will not, cannot, place the least reliance in the use of fair and honorable means. *Fourth.* That the recent developments at New York, Philadelphia, and Cairo, justify us in the worst apprehensions. And finally, that it is always well, in times such as these, to be fully prepared for every contingency; that it is impossible to be too careful of ourselves, or too watchful of those who are our sworn enemies.

While in the South, I wrote several letters to the New York, Boston, and Philadelphia press, and also to the Cincinnati papers, *incog.,* giving them timely warning of the imminent peril of those cities. Whether they were all received and published, I do not know; but certain I am that some of them were, and that, in all probability they were, to a considerable extent, the means of saving those town from destruction. I would also have written to Cairo, but that at that time I did not know who to address. I had been told, by prominent Knights, that there were many of their number in the latter place, and all through Southern Illinois. I was not, however, favored with any of their names. I was also told that there were enough in Southern Indiana to render their Confederate brethren considerable assistance. It was presumed, at one time, that, by the aid of these Hoosier and "Egyptian" Knights, the whole of Southern Indiana and Illinois could be made over to Jeff Davis. In this wild calculation they were very grandly disappointed, as everybody knows. It need not, however, be believed that there are none of the K. G. C. left in those sections, as I shall now proceed to show, from the following statistical account, which I received from the Corresponding Sec. of Jefferson Castle, Kentucky: In New Albany there are about 25 Knights; in Madison 18; in Evansville 15; in Davies county, Ind., 10; in Sullivan county, about 30; in Spencer county, 45; in Vincennes, 14; in Washington county, 10; in Gibson county, 7; in Cairo, Ill., there are, or were, a few weeks ago, 300, and from 100 to 200 in neighboring towns; so that in all there are in the neighborhood of 550 Knights yet in Southern Indiana and Illinois, unless they have lately migrated or renounced the faith. The majority of them, however, are not very dangerous just now without a leader, as they are of what is termed the "small fry." There was one in Evansville, and also one in Princeton, Ind., who *might be feared,* but due notice of their characters having been given to the proper authorities of those places some time since, they have been properly attended to, and will be prevented from committing any overt act. The way in which these resident Knights will do great harm hereafter is in conveying intelligence to the friends of "Southern rights" of the movements of troops and the chances of spoil in various places, which intelligence, in the future, may prove highly important to the rebels. Some of them may also be mean enough to poison their patriotic neighbors, or do sly injury to such of the government troops as they may be convenient to.

Members of the Inner Temple, of the Knights of the Golden Circle are to be scattered all through Missouri, Kentucky, Virginia, and Maryland, for the purpose of harrassing and injuring the friends and soldiers of the Union in every way they can. No particular programme is made out for them, but they are to do whatever they can, in any way, or by any means available. If they can use poison successfully, they will do it; if they can, by false statements, so direct the movements of the United States troops as to cause them a loss or a defeat, they will do that; if they find it convenient to burn a town or destroy a bridge, they will not be condemned by their directors for that act; if they can give the "Knights Gallant" any sure directions for the capture of prizes, etc., they will be highly rewarded and praised for that. In short, they are to make themselves generally useful. But one thing above all others, some one of them is to distinguish himself for, *if he can*, and that is, the assassination of the "Abolition" President.

It matters not whether Maryland and Kentucky go out of the Union or remain in it, they will be, to a very considerable extent, occupied by the worst enemies the government has. The proclamations of the Governors of such states, prohibiting the passage of Confederate troops over their territory, will have about as much effect on the Knights as a moonbeam has on an iceberg in the North pole. They will provide ways and means for the trans-movements of Confederate soldiers without any knowledge of the matter ever reaching the Governor. There are nearly six thousand Knights in Kentucky, about three thousand in Maryland, and a great many in Delaware, and so long as the chief executives of those states do not issue proclamations ordering the disbanding of their castles, yea, and even the execution of those who continue loyal to the Order, just so long will their efforts to prevent treasonable acts be null and void.

Nor is the position of armed neutrality likely to be assumed by some of the Border States to be regarded otherwise than as the most dangerous one they could occupy, for the following conclusive reasons: *First.* Among the most forward of those who enter the "STATE GUARD" will be the members of the Inner Temple of the K. G. C. *Second.* Having secured the state arms, no matter how much they swear to use them only in defense of their state, they will readily and cheerfully employ them in making night forays into Northern borders, in promoting the passage of contraband goods to secessionists, in guarding and protecting our enemies in their midst, or in assisting the passage of secession troops through certain routes in their states to Northern points. There can be no doubt that they would, in many instances, render the

Southern traitors more effective assistance in the capacity of *neutral "State Guards"* than in any other they could serve.

Through many routes lying across Western Kentucky secession forces could be conveyed, in disguised squads, to out-of-the-way places along the Illinois border above Cairo, especially when escorted by Knights in the character of "State Guards." These trans-movements could be effected under cover of the night, in utter ignorance of the Governor of Kentucky. But inasmuch as his Honor, Governor Magoffin, is said to be himself a Knight of the first magnitude, and inasmuch as his indignant refusal to comply with the demands of the Government, with many other of his recent acts, indicate strong sympathy, if not affiliation, with Jeff Davis & Co., it is not at all probable that he would exert himself to the endangering of his personal comfort to ascertain what might be going on everywhere.

Further, while an armed State Guard, largely composed of Inner Templars, would, to say the least, allow Southern soldiers to pass over to Northern borders without interruption, they would repel, with all their might, a Northern detachment that might be in pursuit of Confederate desperadoes. Now, while it is true that there are numbers of sworn enemies to the United States in the Border Slave States, it is also true that there are many warm and devoted friends to the Union in those states. But these latter will stand a very poor chance against the secessionists, from the fact that, although they are largely in the majority, they know not how to compete with the Knights in scoundrelism. In latter times, it seems that a minority of rascals is greatly superior to a majority of honest men. What villains lack in numbers and power, they more than make up in intrigue and activity. It is an historical fact that pirates can easily whip double their number of honorable soldiers. So of the K. G. C. in the Border States: they never fear of success in any of their undertakings where they have but twice their number of Union men to oppose. I will cite a case in point:

In the town of Owensboro', Kentucky, there was a large majority of Union men up to the time of the bombardment of Sumter; but no sooner had the news of that affair reached the place than every Knight in town seized a musket, imbibed a pint or so of the secession element, (whisky,) and paraded up and down the streets, swearing he'd "be d—d if any man dare say *Union* in that locality." On the following evening they called a secession meeting, where all the "good and tried" gathered, with their guns, their pistols, their knives, and, above all, their whisky. Secession speeches were made, cheers for Jeff & Co. were given, groans and curses for Lincoln and the "Abolition" government. A Union man could not find room to breathe freely. Finally, a Vigilance Committee was announced, to be composed of Messrs. So-and-So, (this committee was appointed the evening previous in castle, and was a "Knights' Safety Guard,) and the important duty of driving

"Abolitionists" out of town assigned it. The meeting adjourned, the committee aforesaid imbibed afresh of the "Confederate" element, and went about the exercise of its functions with a remarkable degree of alacrity. They even hunted till midnight to find a "*Union man*," swearing no such individual would find the atmosphere of Owensboro' healthy;" that it would do them good to "run a bayonet through an Abolitionist," etc. Where is the decent man that could withstand such a demonstration as this?

It will be seen, from the expositions of the last few pages, that the enemy of American liberty in the United States is a very wily one; that he is no ordinary enemy, and, therefore, can not be successfully dealt with by ordinary means. The armies of the Union will find the intrigue of the secessionists far more fatal than their steel. While boasting of their bravery and chivalry, they are, at the same time, the most sneaking, contemptible cowards that ever trod the earth. The Southern people were once a very noble people, truly chivalrous and brave. They were so in the days of·Washington, Marion, Sumter; but their glory has vanished in later years, and their bravery is no more. Of course this remark is not meant to be applied universally. There are still brave Southrons, but they are among the few, not the many. Scarcely a single instance is on record where a Southern man, in recent years, has manifested a willingness to meet an antagonist on fair and equal footing. In nearly every modern duel or personal rencounter between a Northern and a Southern man, or between a slave aristocrat and a liberal Southron, we find that the oligarchs have fought on their own plan, with a clear and decided advantage. The brutal attack on Senator Sumner by the fiendish Brooks, the cowardly murder of Senator Broderick, and many other instances of like character, fully and conclusively establish the truth of this statement.

From the very commencement of the secession movement, the disunionists have displayed little else than treachery and cowardice; and they do not hope to attain their ends by good engineering and brave fighting, but by rascality and incendiarism. This is the way they began, and it is the way they intend to finish. They have, at this time, at least a dozen spies North where we have one South; and the great difficulty is, that so many of their agents are residents among us, and have been for years; and while we are depending on them as loyal assistants, and they are making some show in that direction, they are, at the same time, playing into the hands of our enemies in the most skillful and effective manner.

Again, there are the ladies. Who knows what to do with them, or how to manage them? A woman is, at best, a rather unmanageable creature, but a secession lady is especially so. Courtesy, politeness, good breeding, demand that a woman should be kindly, respectfully treated; and the *superior* improvements in modern etiquette, and the extraordinary progress and developments of the crinoline age, demand that we of the masculine gender should keep at a *"respectable distance"* on a *"short acquaintance."* In view of these facts, and in consideration of the importance attached to the character of a female spy, I would suggest the propriety of appointing female vigilance committees in every town and neighborhood, to whom shall be assigned the duty of keeping an eye on their sister visitors from the sunny South, their trunks, skirts, etc. Among other things, it would be well for these female committees to see that no letters from a strange lady, directed to any point South, should go into the post-office unexamined; and this should be especially and particularly attended to where there is good reason for suspicion. The superior judgment of our Northern ladies would of course enable them to conduct their operations in a proper and becoming manner.

I know it seems rather rude, in this age of refinement, to demand a knowledge of the contents of a woman's letter, or of the character of the articles in her trunk; and, more especially, of the amount of *"steel,"* etc., contained in her skirts. But it should be borne in mind that these are war times; that our liberties are at stake; that "eternal vigilance is the price of liberty;" that those who threaten our ruin and the destruction of the country, are aiming to take every dishonest advantage of us; that no condescension is too low for them; and that, therefore, we are fully justifiable in the use of any and every means which has for its object the retardation of their nefarious schemes.

The men who have precipitated this country into civil war have never had any sense of justice, and all their pretensions in that direction are, and ever have been, false. The lofty dignity attributed to Jeff Davis is precisely the same kind of dignity manifested by his father, the devil, in the garden of Eden, when he promised our mother Eve that if she would pluck and eat of the forbidden fruit she and her progeny should be as gods. Conscience, among secessionists, is an obsolete term, if Webster has properly defined it, and, consequently, all appeals to that high moral faculty will have about as much effect in checking their villainous movements as the wind from a hand-bellows would have in retarding the course of a hurricane. When men, such as the leaders of the present rebellion, are successfully met, it must be upon their own ground, and to a very considerable extent, at least, with their own weapons. I admire the high moral tone of the present administration, as manifested in its refusal to allow of the confiscation of the effects of the Southern traitors in Northern states. But while I admire it, and while I would hold it up as an example to the world, under all ordinary circumstances, yet I can but consider it, in the present condition of things, as not only impracticable, but as absolutely suicidal and unjust both to the government and the people of the North. While we stand up in our high moral rectitude, and refuse to touch a single cent's worth of the Southern banditti's property in our midst, they are not only levying upon and appropriating whatever of our effects may chance to be found in their states, and, thief-like, refusing to pay what they honestly owe us, but, as has been shown in preceding pages, are organizing the most effective bands of highway robbers and plunderers to depredate upon Northern soil. Further, they have made all necessary arrangements to send among us their bogus male and female refugees, to act in concert with our own native traitors, as aids and assistants to their hellish desperadoes. So we see, and are bound to admit, that the superior moral position assumed by the government, while it is more than fair for the rebels, is positively oppressive and destructive to us. I presume the extraordinary justice shown the secessionists in this affair is to reward them for the ample service they rendered the nation some time ago, in stealing its treasury, robbing it of its arms, and poisoning such of its officials as were found susceptible. The refusal of the President to allow the Pennsylvania merchants to levy upon the property of Southrons in their state, although undoubtedly well meant, was little better, in consideration of all the facts in the case, than taking the worth of such property immediately out of their pockets. It is the absolute duty of the United States authorities, and of state authorities, to secure and appropriate every dime's worth of the property of the disunionists found north of Mason and Dixon's line; a duty in every sense of the term, morally, religiously, and pecuniarily. Men in revolutionary times, such as these, in successfully opposing an enemy such as we have to meet, must be practical, not theoretical. They must view both sides of every issue, and be able to see justice in more than one light, and as to be applied in more than one direction. A set of men who have been maturing schemes of national robbery and piracy for nearly thirty years are not to be conquered by appeals to something of which they have not the slightest knowledge—conscience. Men who can employ their women to assist in plundering our homes and despoiling our domestic happiness, are not to be affected by the mild principles of Christianity. The bayonet will penetrate them much more effectively than the moral teachings of Christ; a ten-inch columbiad will present far more weighty and convincing arguments to them than the most learned and powerful theologian in the world, and a few dollars taken from their pockets will do more to weaken their diabolical resolutions than all the appeals that could be made to their (o) sense of honor in a century.

As has already been indicated, there are yet several Knights scattered about in various places over the country, and wherever they are, they exert a greater or less influence upon those who immediately surround them. There are many traitors in the North who do not belong to the K. G. C., but they are, in most

instances, the disciples of one or more who live in their neighborhood. For instance, in Carlisle, Sullivan county, Indiana,
there are from fifteen to twenty Jeff Davis subjects, who absorb
the teachings and obey the mandates of a Knight of the Outer
Temple, and he, with them, has repeatedly sworn that if he fights
for anybody, it will be for Jeff Davis. This individual has a rela-
tive in the South that he frequently visits, with whom he is in
regular correspondence, and to whom he transmits the news of
the condition of affairs in Southern Indiana. He often receives
letters enveloped in the secession flag, but the post-master of Carlisle being as scoundrelly a traitor as himself, nothing is said of
the matter. This arch-fiend, not only has his proselytes in Carlisle,
but claims quite a number of followers in various places in Sullivan county. Again, there is, in Davies county, Indiana, a clique
of similar character, governed and controlled by several Knights.
This combination is more powerful than the one in Sullivan, and
once or twice even threatened to mob any company of U. S. volunteers that might be formed in Davies. They concluded not to
do it, however, I believe. There is not the least doubt that, under
the auspices of Drongoole, in Martin, and in some few parts of
Pike counties, there is another traitorous gang of marauders. I
am not thoroughly informed whether there are any combinations
in any other localities along our Southern border, but presume
there are, especially about Madison, New Albany, and Rockport.
The almost universal loyal feeling which prevails in those places,
will, beyond doubt, check any outward displays in favor of the
enemy by the Daviesites; but it need not be presumed that "no
danger," which is always the cry of the over-confident, need be
apprehended from them. They may become "converted" to the
Union doctrine, and join "home guards," or even enlist in the
government service, especially if they can get to be officers, and
still render the most effective assistance to the South.

I had it from prominent Knights, that full and complete arrang-
ments had been made with sundry members in the North, to furnish them important dispatches in the following manner: They,
the Northern members, were to remain in their respective localities, make loud professions of Union sentiments, gather all the
news they could, by telegraph and otherwise, and transmit the
same, through men of their own stripe, from town to town through
the post-offices, until it reached a border town, and here it was to
be conveyed across the line, to the nearest Southern town, and
mailed to the proper persons. Others, again, were to join the U. S.
army, transmit dispatches in a similar manner, create false impressions respecting the movements of Southern troops, etc., and
thereby draw our men into dangerous and destructive snares. Still
others were to join home guards, make sufficient Union noise to prevent suspicion, and, in the meantime, act as secret escorts to Southern scouts, directing them by the proper routes, telling them where

friends were, and by what means they could best accomplish their ends. It will be seen that in all these capacities Northern traitors could yield much assistance to the "Knights Gallant" mentioned in the programme of general movements, given in preceding pages. I also understood that similar arrangements, on a much more extensive and complicated scale, had been made in nearly all the Eastern towns and cities. It was presumed that the city of New York, alone, contained at least five hundred Knights of the Inner Temple; that among them were telegraph operators, post-office clerks, and express agents; that these were of the true and tried, and that there was not the slightest room for doubting their loyalty to the K. G. C. under all circumstances. Many of them were Southern born, and could be relied on to the last extremity. All those who were natives of the North, had been taken to some Southern town and initiated, between New Year's day and the first of March, 1861. I was told that no less than twenty-five were initiated in Baltimore on one evening, every one of whom were of New York. The majority of those of the K. G. C. now living in Border States, especially those in Southern Indiana, Illinois, and Ohio, have been sent out from Southern castles within the last few weeks, *i. e.* just before and immediately after Sumter's bombardment. As I have before stated, they even tried to institute castles in the immediate Northern borders after the Sumter affair, but did not *report favorably.* It was apprehended that in large sections of Indiana, Illinois, Pennsylvania, and New York, no difficulty would be encountered by these Knights' spies, it being presumed that however strong the Union feeling might grow, there would still remain many, not Knights, who would warmly sympathize with the South. I saw in Henderson, Kentucky, a New York drummer who belonged to the Inner Temple, who said that the Southern trade would tie New York city to the South in spite of any efforts on the part of the Administration to keep her loyal. This was said quite recently. We also frequently see it stated in the papers that the Southern people still believe there are many warm friends of "Southern rights" in the North; and however much it may depress the feelings of the Union loving masses, I feel it my duty to tell them that there is even yet too much foundation for this belief. In Indianapolis, Terre Haute, and other places in Indiana; in Cincinnati, Columbus, etc., Ohio; in Philadelphia and other cities in Pennsylvania; in New York and other points, New York State, and, in fact, in nearly every Northern city and town of any consequence, and in many small towns and country neighborhoods, there are numbers of secret agents in almost constant correspondence with various castles and individuals in the South. Many of these send their letters round by by-ways, to prevent their being opened. A few of them are natives, but more of them are "Southern refugees." Beside these, there are several persons who do not belong to the K. G. C. among the leading men of the North, who think more of the South than they do of the government, and in their correspondence they often tell their friends of the Slave States, that the time is rapidly coming when there will be a "great reaction" in the North. Again, there are still a few of our Northern papers that are allowed to talk treason in a sort of round-about way. All these things put together, give the friends of "Southern rights" some grounds for presuming they have considerable sympathy in the North.

The foregoing disclosures and facts indicate that there is much to do in this our great effort to retain our liberties, beside equipping and sending out armies. Those who remain at home have, if anything, the most important labor to perform. To them falls the work of watching spies from abroad and traitors at home; who, however much the more sanguine may be disposed to doubt it, are far more numerous than many have the least idea of. It has frequently been said of late, that overpowering numbers, plenty of bayonets, and the sight of efficient batteries will make Union men, as was the case in Baltimore. Men who reason deeply and have a thorough knowledge of human nature do not talk thus. An overawing military display never did make patriots. It may scare them into submission and an outward manifestation of patriotism; but nothing save *principle* can make a man truly loyal. *Let it be kept constantly before the minds of the people, and let it never be forgotten throughout this great revolutionary struggle, that conquered friends are far more dangerous than unconquered foes.* Wherever it is presumed that a man, or any number of men has any active sympathy with the Southern traitors, such man or men should be either shipped to the rattlesnake den, or hung. There are two or three places in Southern Indiana and Illinois that should be "cleaned out." Carlisle is one of them, and a small town in Davies county, near Washington, is another. Vigilance committees should be more active and keen eyed; night watches should be increased, well armed and kept actively at work, not only in large towns but in small ones. The Southern traitors calculate very largely on the quantities of provisions they will steal by means of the "Knights Gallant," and it is not their intention to operate on large cities, but on small towns and in country neighborhoods, in almost every one of which they will have a greater or lesser number of spies, who will be constantly working in concert with "Northern friends," in furtherance of their schemes. No neighborhood, however insignificant, should be without its regular night patrol after the war fairly commences, because it is the intention of the Knights to make this a war of extermination, and to carry it on in the most savage and destructive manner. As I have before intimated, they do not anticipate a victory by fair means, although the paragraphs of some of their editors indicate great confidence in the superiority of their troops and the invincibleness of their cause. They do not expect to depend upon regular campaigning, but upon any and every destructive and devastative means they can employ. In castle, I have often heard Knights declare that when the war commenced they would never stop until every "Abolitionist" was killed, and all their property turned to the enrichment of the South; that any true "Southern rights" man would delight in secretly cutting their throats, burning their houses, and appropriating their property. Such sentiments as those just quoted may seem so crazy in spirit that thousands will not believe they could have been uttered by any man. Before going South, I would hardly have believed such myself. But it should be borne in mind that the Southern fire-eaters have been becoming more and more affected with the *nigger mania* for several years, and that their sentiments having permeated nearly the whole South, we should not expect to find the people sane on the subject of slavery. They are just about as crazy for slavery as John Brown, Sen., was against it. Hear the following, which is an abstract of a conversation with a Knight of Tennessee.

"Sir, you know we are a peculiar people; that our surroundings are peculiar; and, in the coming struggle, we shall have more than one thing to think of, and more than one thing to do. The circumstances which surround us are such as will harass and perplex us beyond description. In case of a civil war, there can be no doubt of negro insurrections, which will be terrible and appalling; we will be blockaded on every side; we will be scarce of provisions; the European world will be against us; and all these circumstances, taken together, will drive us to the committal of deeds we never would have thought of before. More than this, many of our people—in fact, nearly all of them—have, for years, been nurturing a *deadly hatred* against the anti-slavery men of the North. The number of niggers they have stolen and caused us to lose, the tract war against slavery, the newspaper war against slavery, the pulpit war against slavery, and the political war against slavery, have all combined to make our people hate the North, and once they get a chance at them, by a declaration of war, they will delight in *just butchering them*, shooting them, and burning their *very houses* over their heads, and destroying them in every other way they can." So it will be seen that they honestly believe they have just causes for the committal of their desperate acts.

The people of the South are exceedingly hasty and impetuous. Their climate, their modes of life, etc., tend to render them so. In addition to these considerations, they are very largely mixed with the French and Spanish bloods, which circumstance is by no means calculated to render them less inflammable. We of the North, on the other hand, live in a cooler climate, have vastly different social and domestic institutions, are mostly from the German and English races, and, consequently, are, in disposition,

5

a very different people, as a general thing. I know some native
Southrons are among us, but I have always noticed that a Southern man in the North was by no means a Southern man in the
South. Of these facts, the Southern people are generally aware.
They also know that we are a more self-reliant people than they;
that we are duly conscious of our superior strength and wealth;
that we are less suspicious of anything evil happening us than
they are; that we are somewhat slower on the move, and that,
consequently, considerable advantage will be gained over us by
sudden, unexpected movements, in remote and unguarded places.
Their night forays and plundering expeditions—and they anticipate many—are all to be conducted on what they term the "Marion" or "Swamp Fox" plan. A party of mounted "Knights
Gallant" are to collect at some point along Mason and Dixon's
line, make a descent upon a corn-growing neighborhood, surprise
some old farmer, take his wagon and team, load up with corn, and
strike for the river. Once there, they will convey their plunder
across, in skiffs and flats, to Southern soil, where a previously
posted guard, with servants, conveyances, etc., will be prepared to
receive them. In the mean time, if the farmer wakes, and is about
to detect them, they will set fire to some of his property, and
thereby distract his attention; or, if he comes too close upon them,
will shoot him, and let him go. In other instances, it will be
arranged with some of the "faithful" to have the farmer and his
family leave home on some particular and designated occasion,
when the same operation can be carried on more conveniently.

Again, it is the intention of the K. G. C. to send large detach-
ments of the mounted "Knights Gallant," armed with rifles,
swords, and short arms, to attack and harass such weaker portions
of the United States army as may be convenient to them. This
kind of fighting suits the young bloods of the South far better
than any other. There is just enough of risk and romance about
it to inspire them, and there is no doubt that they will vie with
each other in the performance of extraordinary feats, and the
achievement of grand little victories. To fully prepare them for
this species of warfare, they have, for some time, been practicing
race targeting. This is accomplished by first preparing a circu-
itous race-course, of small circumference—say a quarter of a
mile—then arranging targets, to the number of six to twelve; after
which the "chivalry" mount their fleet horses and ride around
the ring at a rapid speed, firing with revolvers or Miniés at the
targets in succession. This is very grand sport for the "Knights
Gallant," while, at the same time, it gives them the very best of
dragoon drill.

Now, in order to meet this extensive guerrilla arrangement successfully, I would suggest the formation of similar companies, and
the practice of a similar drill, in the North. We have young men
just as active and as brave as any in the South, or elsewhere; we

have horses, plenty of them, as good as were ever saddled; and we have the means and the will to make this kind of service equally as effective as the Southern people can. If the Government will not authorize it, let it be done on individual responsibility. It should be done; it *must* be done, if we intend to save our homes, our lives, and our liberties.

In looking round over the country, since I returned North, 1 find the means of defense, as a general thing, very inferior to what they should be. I also notice, as before intimated, that the Northern people are nowhere vigilant enough. I would, therefore, again enforce the great, the urgent necessity of stricter vigilance, and more thorough, systematic means of defense. The citizens of the Free States seem disposed to make large deductions from the probability of any aggressive measures by the South, on the supposition that the prevention of negro insurrections will occupy the "chivalry" to such an extent as to render such measures inimical to home interests. From this argument, although to one not acquainted with the Southern character it would seem very forcible, much weight is subtracted by the fact that secessionists nowhere bear the reputation of being prudent and considerate, *i. e.*, the masses. It is true that such men as Cobb and Floyd have displayed a little forethought in the way they prepared for the revolution; but it is a fact well known to zoölogists, that almost every kind of animal, whether intelligent or automatic, knows how to provide for its own wants. It is also a fact, of which almost every one is aware, that when a hog is hungry, and can not obtain corn honorably, he will enter the crib and take it, if the door is left open. Mr. Buchanan left Uncle Sam's crib door wide open during the whole of the term he had the keeping of it, and, of course, there was every opportunity for the shoats in the public barn-yard to help themselves. I see no great display of genius or "far-sightedness" in this, because thieving is an instinct belonging even to the lowest animals. The great majority of the Southern people, however, are not Cobbs, nor Floyds, nor Davises, by a long distance, either in point of talent or coolness. They are, as has been stated, a people of moderate intellectual caliber, and largely preponderating animal passions, which circumstances, in consideration of the highly exciting influences surrounding them, utterly forbids the possibility of anything like an ordinary display of wisdom. Negro insurrections they have expected from the beginning, and so far from its having had the effect to cool the secession fever, it has only increased it.

Notwithstanding the fact that they are fully convinced that they are, to say the least, the immediate cause of all their own trouble, yet, as that trouble becomes more and more aggravated, they become more and more intensified in their deadly hatred toward the Northern people. It is utterly impossible for me to describe the fierce, fiendish revengefulness I have seen depicted in their countenances while conversing with them of national affairs. This unnatural feeling toward us was not general, by any means, even in the Gulf States, until engendered there by the Knights, and, until then, was scarcely visible in the Border States. But it is everywhere now, where a castle exists; and as the civil war approaches, by their incessant efforts, night and day, they continue to spread and intensify it. If I am asked the reason for the existence of such a state of affairs, I can only give, as my reply, what is my honest opinion: the Southern people have gone mad on the Slavery Question. The large majority of them seem to be perfectly reckless of the present, entirely regardless of the future; while there are a few of the leading revolutionary spirits, in almost every locality, who seem to think the cause of secession so holy, and the people of the South so invincible, that no power on earth, nor all the powers of the world combined, could conquer them, under any circumstances.

The foregoing considerations, together with the exciting promptings of hunger and want, consequent upon the Government blockade, render it morally certain that the work I have described as having been assigned the K. G. will be done, both as a work of revenge and of necessity, even by those who have long lived by us as our neighbors and brethren on the borders, and who have not undergone that long, thorough course of training in the tactics of the Knights which their more distant secession relatives of the Cotton States have. Let it not, therefore, be presumed by the hopeful friends of freedom in the North, that "there is no danger;" but, on the other hand, let danger be fully expected, and prepared for in the most thorough manner; danger of every description, both at home and from abroad.

CHAPTER IX.

YANCEY AND TOOMBS—THE SLAVE TRADE AND FILLIBUSTERING— NORTHERN SYMPATHIZERS WITH THE LATTER—THE "ABOLITION" SCARECROW—THE LECOMPTON SWINDLE THE WORK OF THE K. G. C. —SIMILARITY OF THAT FRAUD WITH SECESSION OPERATIONS— THE IMPETUS GIVEN THE SECESSION MOVEMENT BY THE REPUBLICAN LEADERS IN 1860—THE BRECKINRIDGE PARTY A SECESSION ORGANIZATION.

It will be remembered that Mr. Yancey said, after the withdrawal of his state from the Union, that he had been a secessionist for thirty years. It will also be remembered that it was charged that Mr. Toombs said, in a speech he delivered in Con-

gress a few years ago, that he expected to see the day when he
could call the roll of his slaves at the foot of Bunker Hill Monu-
ment. These remarks will not be wondered at when it is revealed
that the men from whom they emanated are the oldest members
of the Southern Rights' Club now living. Yancey paid, out of
his own pocket, over ten thousand dollars to equip secret slavers,
between the years 1834 and 1840. Toombs, who is presumed to
be the wealthiest man in Georgia, donated, from time to time, for
the same purpose, over twenty thousand dollars. In many instances it was not necessary to purchase or build a ship, but
merely to buy or hire the master. Of the six kidnapping vessels
sent out between 1834–'40, five were Yankee crafts, owned by
Yankee captains; and the whole three plying during 1856 were
New York vessels. Thus it will be seen that the Southern people
have some reason for saying that a Yankee can easily be induced
to sell anything he has, even to his honor; that among the Northerners there is no such thing as principle.

That greatest of all scarecrows, "*Abolitionism*," has been the
pretext, during the past few years, for every species of secession scoundrelism. A man who moved to Kansas Territory and
favored the Free State ticket was an *Abolitionist;* the man who
honestly believed that slavery was the creature of local law,
and that the Constitution of the United States did not carry and
protect it everywhere, was an *Abolitionist;* the man who denied
the constitutional right of secession, or the right of one state to
destroy the whole government, was an *Abolitionist;* and, finally,
in latter days, the man who sustains the Constitution and upholds
the stars and stripes, is an *Abolitionist.* Just at this latter junc-
ture, the Northern secessionists, with few exceptions, call a halt,
having been hitherto apparently *blind* respecting the direct and
legitimate tendency of their promotion of "Southern rights," and
their opposition to "*Abolitionism.*" With the exceptions of those
contemptible specimens of humanity, Vallandigham, of Ohio,
and Jesse D. Bright, of Indiana, there are few politicians in the
Northwest who are not now, in Southern eyes, what they so
recently abhorred, "*Abolitionists.*" The real Abolition party of
the North was so insignificant a political element that no sensible
Southern man had the slightest fears of danger from it. It only
needed to have been let alone to have died so dead that it would
never more have been heard of. While conversing with the Hon.
Archie Dixon, of Kentucky, some months ago, he remarked to me:
"We could have always managed the Abolitionists had it not been
for the Knights of the Golden Circle in the South, and their ac-
complices in the North. The great Northwestern States always
contained a wholesome conservative majority until the Yancey
school, in the Slave States, and the Buchanan school, in the Free
States, undertook to construe the Constitution into a pro-slavery
document."

Who desires better proof of the determination of the secessionists, North and South, not to allow the "Abolition" fire to go down, than the course which was taken by them to force the great Lecompton swindle through Congress at its 35th session? That swindle was the legitimate concoction of the K. G. C., and was produced and presented in the manner that it was, for the sole purpose of strengthening the free-soil element in the North, and dividing the Democratic party. Notwithstanding all the "outrages" that were committed in "Bleeding Kansas," the conservative people of the Free States had elected "Granny" Buchanan on the principle of non-intervention, by a large majority, in 1856; and it was plainly obvious that something a little stronger than the repeal of the Missouri Compromise and the doctrine of Popular Sovereignty was required to thoroughly "abolitionize" the North. The so-called Constitution, framed by the K. G. C. Convention at Lecompton, was considered the very thing that would accomplish the work. In electing delegates to that Convention, the same "coercive" appliances were used to secure the success of the pro-slavery ticket that are now used to elect delegates to a secession convention, and the same fraud and trickery were manifested in its deliberations that have since characterized the secret sessions of every secession body that has convened. It is also true, and I here record it as a matter of history, that the same class of arguments was used, both by the K. G. C. of the South and their truckling followers in the North, to prove the legality of the Lecompton Constitution as is now used, by the same individuals, to prove the legitimacy of a secession ordinance.

How any man with one particle of honesty or consistency could come before the intelligent masses of the Free States advocating the claims of a presidential platform, the very framers of which had been, more or less, engaged in the Lecompton secession scheme, is an enigma, the unraveling of which I confess myself totally incapable of performing.

While the world stands, and the people continue to think, there is one thing which will remain a lasting disgrace to the Republican party. I allude to the assistance they rendered the Breckinridge secessionists, in the campaign of 1860, in the North. Although totally ignorant of the secrets of the K. G. C., by whom Mr. B. was nominated, yet they did far more to popularize his ticket north of Mason and Dixon's line, than the secessionists themselves. All the senatorial speeches made against Douglas by such men as Benjamin and Jeff Davis, were eagerly sought for, and vigorously circulated, by the leading Republicans throughout the country. Further, the same partisans used almost superhuman efforts to swell the numbers at all the secession ratification meetings that were called, from time to time, in the Northern States, during the campaign. While it was utterly impossible for the Republicans and Secession Democrats to harmonize on a single principle, they agreed to unite in their mutual hatred of Douglas. Of course it was to the interest of the Republicans that the Democratic party should be divided; and, according to the rules of political warfare, there is nothing wrong in one party taking advantage of the disconcerted condition of another, to secure a victory. But I apprehend there is an honorable way of profiting by such advantages. The Republicans must have seen that the Breckinridge ticket was a secession ticket, and that, consequently, the favoring of it, either directly or indirectly, was the promotion of rebellion and civil war. To have acted honorably in the matter, therefore, would have been to discuss and enforce the merits of their own platform and candidates, and let both Breckinridge and Douglas tickets entirely alone, especially the former. The Republicans certainly were the more natural friends and allies of the Douglas men, as it regarded the maintenance of the Union and the enforcement of the laws, as has been fully proven since the outbreak of the present revolution.

I was myself a Republican, and a warm supporter of the Republican platform, but never could get the consent of my consistency to encourage the secession ticket. The real criminality of such an encouragement, however, never fully appeared to me until I traveled South, and there, both in castle and out doors, heard the K. G. C. congratulating themselves over the "valuable" assistance rendered them by the "Abolitionists" of the North.

The Republican party has a platform of which it may justly be proud, and has done many highly estimable things; but the promotion of the secession ticket in the Free States during the campaign of 1860 was not one of those things. Should it survive the present storm, and again present its claims to the people of this government, let it never be guilty of another so gross and fatal a crime as this was.

In due keeping with the manner in which the K. G. C. tried to palm the Lecompton swindle on the honest-thinking masses, in 1857-'58, and in precisely the same spirit in which they have since conducted the secret sessions of their secession conventions, and forced their secession ordinances upon their fellow citizens, we now find them conducting all their present diabolical schemes. Having assumed the capacity of "Confederate" officers, and having deprived the people, by armed mob suasion, of all their power, they form a bogus government, establish bogus laws, and, by the most inhuman, brutal means, force the rightful sovereigns of the land to obey them. Wherever they have the power, they arraign, try, and hang, as a traitor, a man, for merely asserting his preference of the United States Government, they confiscate and plunder the property of those who refuse to take up arms against their country; they beat and mercilessly abuse a man for merely saying that the fanatics of the North and South are equally to blame for the present unhappy state of affairs; they, in their fiendish madness, even condescend to drive innocent, helpless women from their homes, not allowing them. in many instances, to take their own ward-robes with them; they steal all the U. S. property which they can appropriate to their own use, and destroy that which is not avail-able; they burn and blow up bridges and public buildings; they issue bogus warrants for the arrest of such sterling patriots as Nelson and Johnson; they concoct secret schemes to arm the se-cessionists of such states as Kentucky and Maryland, to the end of dragging them forcibly out of the Union; they locate secret agents in the Border States to assist in conveying arms, provisions. etc., into the seceded states, to destroy lives and property, and violate female virtue: they send agents to Europe to misrepresent the true state of affairs in this country, and to induce foreign powers to assist them in destroying this government. Is there not a day of RETRIBUTION?

CHAPTER X.

WHAT THE K. G. C. INTEND TO DO WITH THEIR GOVERNMENT SHOULD THEY SUCCEED IN THEIR DESIGNS—THE RENEWAL OF THE SLAVE TRADE—THE REASONS WHY NOTHING IS SAID OF SLAVE TRADE NOW —THE ESTABLISHMENT OF AN ARISTOCRACY—THE WAR OF 1861— NORTHERN DEPRECIATION OF SOUTHERN STRENGTH.

HAVING traced the movements of the S. R. C. from 1834 to 1855, and having considered its metamorphosis, at the latter period, into the K. G. C., and its subsequent movements in the political arena up to the present day, I will now lay before the reader's mind the anticipations of the secessionists in the future.

In the first place, the Knights have, by no means, forgotten their original pet idea of slave stealing. This was the substratum upon which their mud-sills were laid in the beginning, and, although obscured by the foam of the secession cauldron for the present, will be brought out in full relief, in case the secessionists succeed in the establishment of a new government. Every member of the Inner Temple of the K. G. C. is an advocate of the slave trade, and so soon as opportunity is afforded, will make zealous, per-sistent efforts for its re-establishment. The castle was divided into an Outer and Inner Temple, in the first place, in order that there might be, in the former, a place of rendezvous for secessionists, whether for or against the foreign black traffic, and in the latter a place of refuge for the known and proved friends of the slave piracy. Whenever you come in contact with an Inner Templar, and broach the subject of the foreign traffic, he talks to you in the following style:

" We, who have made the subject of slavery a study, know that it is an institution which must be either on the increase or decrease; that it must either continue to grow in extent and power, or ultimately become extinct. We already have more territory than we have boys to cultivate it in the proper manner. There are thousands of acres of the very best of cotton land in many of the Gulf States untouched. The Border Slave State supply of negroes has never been anything like equal to the Cotton State demand. But further, we intend to have Cuba, Mexico, and certain portions of Central America; and, consequently, there will be a great *increase* in the demand for slaves. How are we to get them, otherwise than by a resort to Africa? By going there, we can get them much cheaper, and in greater quantities, than we can in any part of the United States. Besides this, we can procure *better* slaves in Africa than we can in America. The 'niggers' we get in the Border Slave States are generally very inferior as servants, and especially so as field-hands. Many of them are, in consequence of their large admixture of Anglo-Saxon blood, lazy, stubborn, and insubordinate. They are, also, shorter lived than the genuine African, and can not endure the labor in the cotton fields as he does. So far as the moral part of the negro traffic is concerned, there certainly is less sin in buying and selling the genuine Guinea kinky-head than there is in trading in those of their American descendants, whose veins contain much of our own blood, if there be any sin in it at all."

These are the arguments that the Inner Templars present in favor of its re-establishment; and if the institution of slavery be right, or if it be even tolerable, in a republic, they are unanswerable. I have cited them to show the tendency of the anticipated Southern Government, and to prove that, should they once cut loose from the United States, the fire-eaters will never rest easy until they have renewed the slave piracy.

Perhaps it will here be asked, why the Montgomery Congress voted so largely against the introduction of this doctrine into the Confederate Constitution, if they really indorsed it? The following are the reasons: *First.* They knew the Border Slave States, whose main dependence was the Southern negro-market, never could be induced to ratify a constitution which allowed of the African slave trade. *Second.* They were convinced that it would be folly to hope to secure the sympathy of any European power under such circumstances. In their then weak condition they knew that to renew the foreign traffic would be to shut out all hope of the successful attainment of their designs. But no sooner will their government be established, than all their energies will be turned to that end.

In the second place, the leaders of this rebellion have never anticipated, what many persons have supposed they did, the establishment of a government composed exclusively of the Southern States. They know full well that such a government could not long exist. It has been their intention, from the beginning, to secure the annexation of all the great Middle and Northwestern States, or, at least, a great portion of them. Without the co-operation of those Northern States which lie along the lower Ohio and Mississippi, their produce trade would be seriously impaired, and likely to be suspended at any time. Of the Southern and Northwestern States they intended to form what they term a limited aristocracy—a government which has been, for years, considered by the nabobs of the South as far better and more permanent than a republic. Many of the leading citizens of the South have told me that they had regarded the present form of the American Government as a failure, for a long time; that it had, almost from the very beginning, manifested a great lack of power and efficiency. This idea may truly seem strange, when it is remembered that Thomas Jefferson, a Southern man, was the father of Democracy; that he, with almost all the Southern statesmen of his time, waged an uncompromising war against the more centralizing doctrines of Federalism; and that, from his day to 1856, the stronghold of Democracy has been the South. The aristocracy alluded to is to be governed by a dictator, who may hold his office for life, unless deposed by the Congress. None but the wealthy are to be allowed a vote, and no one who is not known to have large interests in slave property is to be allowed to hold any office; and none but the most genuine of the *chivalry* are to be allowed a seat in the Confederate Parliament. These latter, when proved and chosen, are, like the dictator, to be allowed to continue in office for life, and when they die, their successors are to be chosen from among their descendants. In short, the intention of the secessionists is to have a more powerful monarchy than that of England. The steps toward its consummation are, however, to be gradual. By thus wresting the power of the government from the people, and placing it in the hands of the aristocracy, they could re-open the slave-trade, and carry on aggressive and acquisitive wars to any desirable extent.

What change may have been effected in the designs of the K. G. C. since the unanimous uprising of all the Free States, and the apparent division in many of the Border Slave States, I know not, but certain I am that they still contemplate the establishment of a government vastly more centralized than the one we now live under. Without the constant aid of a standing army and an efficient navy, no power composed of Slave States can, for a day, maintain itself.

Thus it will be seen that the present revolution is not only intended to sunder the bonds that bind the Union together, but to prove the experiment of self-government a failure, and to crush at once, and forever, the last remaining hope of freedom to the world. The military discipline so strictly enforced in the "Articles of War" promulgated by the "American Legion" of the K. G. C., has strict reference to the continual use which is to be made of it hereafter. No candidate is admitted into the Order without he declares, most emphatically, that he will "strictly observe" these "Articles of War, as promulgated by the Legion."

The question now to be asked by every true American citizen is—Shall I, while life remains, submit to the establishment of a power which has for its sole object the destruction of that liberty which cost the Revolutionary fathers their fortunes and their lives?

The American Government is now threatened by an enemy far more dangerous than any it has hitherto contended with. All the foreign powers of the world combined would not be so much to be dreaded as the internal foe we now have to contend with. There is, therefore, no time to be spent in foolish, timid regrets; no hours to be wasted in deploring the "condition of the country," but every moment and every power is to be unreservedly given to the most vigorous action. The man who does not prefer death to the loss of his liberty and the destruction of the institutions of such a country as ours, is unworthy the name and privileges of an American citizen, and unfit for any other society than that of South Carolina. I have no patience with those persons who are always regretting this war, and longing for peace. The war is one of the greatest of necessities, and no permanent peace can be rationally hoped for but through the successful use of the rifles and bayonets of the United States troops. The man who cannot see this is either a fool or a cowardly traitor. The idea advanced by a few that it would be better to "*let the South alone*" than to shed the blood of *our brethren*, or sacrifice our own lives and fortunes, if it be honestly declared, can come from none other than the most ignorant and short-sighted of men. Let us suppose, for a moment, that the South were "let alone;" all the lower Mississippi commerce is under its supreme control; the Southern aristocracy can exact just such duties of us as they please, and we must submit, or else be involved in a fight; the K. G. C. can carry forward their acquisitive wars southwardly, and re-open the slave trade, and we dare not open our mouths; and, worst of all, we will ever be regarded by them as the most contemptible cowards in the world. This is already the case, to a very considerable extent; and no hope need be indulged of securing even ordinary respect among them but by administering to them such a chastisement as shall make them remember us.

The present revolution cannot be more productive of suffering and privations than the first one was. Our fathers began the war for their liberties with an empty treasury, few men, few arms, and scarcely any navy at all. We, on the other hand, have a full treasury, a large surplus of men, more provisions than we can consume, plenty of arms, and can soon have an efficient navy. Who, then, shall stand back and cry "peace," or counsel inactivity and delay in this our day of peril?

As to the shedding of "brother's blood," I have this to say; he who lifts his traitorous arm to strike at the American government, be he brother or stranger, is justly deserving of death, and no tears should be shed over his grave. If every man, women, and child in the South has to die, it were far better than to allow the union of these states to be destroyed. The dissolution of the American Union is the destruction of the whole North American continent. The idea of the existence of two governments in this country, so opposite to each other as those which would result from a division of the Northern from the Southern sections, is the most nonsensical of all absurdities, and can only be conceived in the brain of a political idiot. The man who has heretofore enjoyed the benefits of the best government on earth, and who now seeks to destroy it by making war upon it, is worse than any foreign enemy.

The political aristocrats of the South, although now pretending to the world that they only wish to be "let alone," are really aiming at the subjugation of the North. Nearly ever since the birth of the republic, they have had almost complete control of it, and are now stung to the quick by the consciousness that the Northern States have at last shown a disposition to take a hand in its management. The politicians of the South have always believed that the people of the Free States were "too ignorant, cowardly, and selfish" to have a controlling voice in the halls of legislation. They have so long fostered this idea that they have, finally, come to the conclusion that all that is grovelling and degrading in human nature belongs to the North. Whereas, on the other hand, all that is ennobling and great is indigenous to the South. They "have all the talent, bravery, and generosity;" we have all the ignorance, cowardice, and selfishness. To use a Hoosier phrase, *a sound thrashing* is really the only thing that can ever induce the fire-eaters to correct these views, and the sooner it is administered the better.

The Southern people never had a proper appreciation of our superior industrial and educational institutions. Their descendancy from "noble" stock, their inheritance of "sacred" relics, and their absolvence from all kinds of labor have, in their estimation, elevated them far above the "menials" of the North, and given them a rightful claim to the management of this government. Northern courage and Northern bayonets will remove these false notions—nothing else will.

For years the people of the Free States have, for the sake of preserving peace with their *brethren* of the South, humbled themselves in the very dust before the altar of slavery, and displayed a subserviency which is even sickening to contemplate. No wonder they concluded that one Southern man could whip from five to a dozen Northerners, when, with a population hardly one-fifth as great as ours, they have had almost the entire control of the government from its infancy up. Let us redeem our character, and establish our just claims, at every hazard.

CHAPTER XI.

THE MILITARY CHARACTER OF THE K. G. C.—"GEORGE WASHINGTON LAFAYETTE BICKLEY"—WHAT THE SOUTH CAN DO; WHAT WE MUST DO, ETC.

As I have before intimated, the Knights of the Golden Circle are "some military." Ever since 1855, when that lofty specimen of Boone county "chivalry," "George Washington Lafayette Bickley," applied all the powers of his *master* genius to the improvement and superior organization of the Order, the Knights have practiced regular military drill. For his untiring efforts in this regard, the said George Washington Lafayette Bickley has been created president and commander-in-chief of the "American Legion." The object of the military exercises, or, as they are commonly called, "Articles of War," was to prepare for the "impending crisis." Every castle is, in truth, a regular military company, the State Legions are brigades, and the American Legion is an army. Now, when we come to consider that thousands of castles have been drilling two and three times per week, for several years, we must at once acknowledge that their influence in the present revolution will be considerable.

However much persons may be disposed to ridicule the idea of any just apprehension of danger from the military operations of the K. G. C., I can assure them that they will prove a more formidable foe than any outsider has yet presumed. Their long course of training and preparation, their well-matured, deep-laid plans, and their unscrupulous dishonesty, render them capable of effecting far more than any one not acquainted with their organization would expect of them.

The Knights of the Golden Circle are the secessionists proper, and their history is the history of secession. From a small and insignificant band of kidnappers and fillibusters, they have gradually increased their numbers until they are to be counted by thousands in the Southern States of the Union, and by dozens in the Border Free States. Many of these latter are at this time in Philadelphia, Boston, New York, Albany, Cincinnati, Indianapolis, New Albany, Evansville, Cairo, and other border cities. As I have before said, they are the most dangerous of enemies. Some of them being native born, are not suspicioned. The sign of recognition and the response are never given in a Free State, unless the parties giving them know each other well, and are so situated that their communications will not be detected. They may be justly suspicioned, however, from the following expressions, all of which are knightish: "The South only wants her rights;" "Better let them go, than involve ourselves in a war which will cost us more than the South is worth;" "O, dear me! the EXPENSES of this war!" "What will the people say when it comes to paying the heavy taxes?" "The South can never be *subjugated!*" "I never will enlist to fight my *brethren* of the South;" (*brethren* means brethren in the real knightish sense;) "The country's in an awful condition—we'll never be as we were, again." Sometimes an editor of the Knights' school ventures to condemn the "*mobocracy of the North,*" without saying anything of the mobbing proclivities of the South. At other times, as in the case of the editor of the I. S. G., he gives Webster's definition of the term SUBJUGATE, and then, as his only comment, asks the question, "Can eleven States, with a population of three millions of people, *ever be subjugated?*" Let every one who talks thus be closely watched.

In conversing with many hopeful friends of the Union, since my return from the South, I find the confidence in the superior numbers of the loyal troops, and the greater wealth of the North, entirely too great. I also notice that the numbers, power, and resources of the South are too much underrated. The impression, in fact, seems to be entirely too general, that the secessionists, in consequence of their limited means, scarcity of provisions, inferior numbers, and unholy cause, can endure but a short time. I am truly sorry that this idea has obtained to the extent that it has, calculated as it is, in its very nature, to prove more or less disastrous to the cause of the Union.

In the first place, as has been shown, the Confederate States have nearly all the arms contained in the Government arsenals in the early part of 1860, to which, by an arrangement made in the early part of the spring of 1861, have been added a heavy cargo of the latest and most improved European arms—about twenty thousand; and having seized nearly all the Southern forts, they have secured the greater number of our best, heaviest ordnance, and, therefore, are even better supplied in those regards than we are. In the second place, they have more provisions than has generally been supposed. During the whole of the winter and spring of 1861, steamboats and flats have been employed by the score in conveying the heaviest loads of provisions from the great Northwestern States; and from what I have seen and heard in New Orleans, and other river towns, I have not the least doubt that many of the principal cities of the South have provisions enough stored away to supply their citizens several years. In addition to this, every effort will now be made to increase the corn and wheat crops in all the Southern States. For a time, at least, they will forget King Cotton, and pay more attention to Emperor Corn. Further, the Confederates will, without doubt, make the strongest efforts to put those stealing schemes, described in previous pages, into vigorous execution, many of which will, in all probability, succeed, on their immediate borders. In the third place, respecting numbers, they can, without any doubt, muster two hundred thousand fighting men into the field—men of the most desperate and reckless character, who care less for life than they do for a meal's victuals; men of the rough, lower Mississippi order, who have, almost from childhood, been accustomed to murder and bloodshed; men who, although naturally cowards, would rather die a thousand times than have the name of being whipped. In the fourth and last place, as to the cause, the leaders of this great rebellion are fully conscious that, with them, the issue is life or death: that, if conquered, their lives will be terminated in the most shameful manner, and their names handed down to all coming generations as traitors of the blackest stamp; that their children, after them, for many generations, will be disgraced by the deeds of their sires, and that their names will never be mentioned in history or spoken of by men otherwise than as are the names of Arnold and Burr.

Reflections such as these are the most powerful incentives to bold and determined action that can be presented to human pride and ambition anywhere, and, to the aristocratic leaders of the South, they will prove especially so. The struggle, on their part, therefore, will be powerful and desperate; such a struggle as could be manifested by men in no other condition or circumstances. Every effort in the field, every stratagem which they are capable of inventing, and every species of incendiary destruction, will be applied in the most vigorous manner. Meantime, the history of the first American Revolution should not be forgotten. It should be remembered that in strength and resources the American colonies were vastly inferior to the government of Great Britain, and yet we conquered our independence. Let none of the revolutionary lessons of the past be overlooked. It is never a good policy to undervalue the strength and the chances of a foe, if one would be sure of a victory. On the other hand, it is far better to overestimate them. The greatest gold mines in the world are found by looking downward, not upward, and it is always dangerous in passing through a wood to overlook the stones and stubbs in gazing intently at the spreading tops of the tall trees.

But while we concede to the South all that is due it, in the way of strength, facilities, and courage, let us not forget our own power. Nor should we forget the glory of the cause in which we have enlisted: the preservation of this great government, and the perpetuity of our liberties. As with the secessionists, so it is with us, either a matter of life or death, both as a nation and as a people. The world has, for years, been looking to this Republic as the great beacon-light of liberty; the crowned heads of Europe have been long regarding the land of Columbia with jealousy and envy, hoping and praying that our great experiment of self-government might prove a failure. In the mean time, our glorious example has enkindled a burning desire for liberty in the hearts of the people of every surrounding nation, and caused them to revolutionize their despotisms, destroy their feudalisms, modify their monarchies, and improve their aristocracies. The great ball of freedom which our fathers set rolling, has even reached the very heart of old hierarchal Rome, and, by the master-strokes of the immortal GARIBALDI, the Papal throne has been shaken to its very center, and tyrants have been made to quake at the rapid strides of the Genius of Liberty. Our own glorious America has advanced in civilization, in science, arts, improvements, and wealth, to an extent unequaled anywhere or at any time in the world's history: the American flag has become an emblem of glory and protection wherever it waves, whether on land or sea, and the American citizen is honored and respected by all nations of people.

The memories of the Revolutionary fathers, their unprecedented trials and unequaled victories, have not yet become extinct, nor their invigorating influence lost. Our gray-haired sires and aged mothers, as they totter on the verge of the grave, with their souls weighed with despair, and their hearts pierced with regret, turn with feeble though earnest voice, and entreat us to maintain inviolate the rich inheritance bequeathed us by the GRANDSIRES of Seventy-six; our wives, our sisters, our children, with their souls fraught with the remembrance of past blessings, demand of us a continuance of them in future. And, last and greatest of all, GOD, who cleft the waters of the Red Sea, and rolled them to the right hand and to the left, causing his liberated children to walk safely and surely from under the galling yoke of Egypt's tyrant to the wilderness of freedom; GOD, who fought the battles of Israel, and secured to it the land of promise; GOD, who liberated the *world* from sin by the gift of his only-begotten Son; GOD, who nerved the arm of the immortal Luther to the breaking of the Papal chains of Europe and the defense of religious freedom; GOD, who directed the Puritan fathers from under the oppressive hand of Britain to the wilderness of North America; GOD, who heard the prayers of WASHINGTON, fought the battles of American Independence, secured to us civil and religious liberty, and gave to us this great land, with its innumerable, invaluable blessings; GOD, who has always been the friend of FREEDOM, and the foe of oppression, commands us to MOVE FORWARD in defense of the right, the maintenance of our government, and the vindication of its flag. These are *our* incentives, and while they are not calculated to render us so desperate, brutal, and blood-thirsty as those which incite the followers of *Lucifer,* yet they are fraught with that patriotic glory, virtuous enthusiasm, and holy luster which render the soldier under their influence invincible. Then, let every one of the thousands who are marching under the BANNER OF THE FREE be fully imbued with the great fact that he is fighting in the cause of humanity and the cause of GOD.

THE END.

THE RITUAL

KNIGHTS OF THE GOLDEN CIRCLE.

There are three Degrees to the Order; the first ilitary, the second Financial, the third Governmental.

The ritual of the First Degree contains little of special importance. We will here premise that the reading of the Ritual is entirely unintelligible except by the aid of keys, a great many numerical figures being substituted for words. We are in possession of the keys, and, in what we publish of the Rituals, we shall give it just as we find it, putting into parentheses the meaning of the figures. The two following paragraphs are from the Obligation taken in the First Degree, the words of the first being spoken by the Treasurer, and those of the second by an officer called the Captain:

Treasurer: Gentlemen, we must now tell you that the first field of our operations is 2 (Mexico;) but we hold it to be our duty to offer our services to any Southern State to repel a Northern army. We hope such a contingency may not occur. But whether the Union is reconstructed or not, the Southern States must foster any scheme having for its object the Americanization and Southernization of 2 (Mexico,) so that in either case our success will be certain.

Captain. Under the laws of 2 (Mexico,) every emigrant receives from the State authorities a grant of 640 acres of land. Under a treaty closed with 3, (Manuel Doblado, Governor of Guanajuato,) on the 11th of February, 1860, we are invited to colonize in 2, (Mexico) to enable the best people there to establish a permanent government. We agree to introduce a force of 16,000 men, armed, equipped and provided, and to take the field under

6

the command of   (Manuel Doblado, Governor of Guanajuato,)
who agrees to furnish an equal number of men to be officered by
K. G. C.'s.   To cover the original expenses of arming our forces,
there is mortgaged to our Trustees the right to collect one-half the
annual revenues of 4, (Guanajuato) until we are paid the sum of
$840,000.   As a bonus there is also ceded to us 355,000 acres of
land.   The pay of the army is the same as the regular army of
2, (Mexico) which is about one-eighth more than that of the
United States.   To secure this there is mortgaged to us all the
public property of 4, (Guanajuato) amounting in taxable value to
$23,000,000.   3 (Manuel Doblado, Governor of Guanajuato) is
now there, making arrangements for our reception.   We shall
cross over as soon as possible, after our national troubles are settled.

I will now give you the signs, grips, password, and token of the
First Degree of the K. C. G.   (Of course a misprint for K. G. C.)
This Degree has a name, which I may now give you—it is the
"1," (Knight of the Iron Hand.)   The first great sign of the
Order is thus made, 7, (Hands open, palms touching and resting
on the top of the head, fingers pointed upwards.)   The answer to
this is 8 (open hands touching shoulder where epaulettes are
worn; elbows close to the side.)   These are battle-field signs, and
are not to be used under ordinary circumstances.   The common
sign of recognition is 9 (right forefinger drawn across upper lip
under nose, as " rubbing.)   The answer 10, (with forefinger and
thumb of left hand take hold of left ear.)   To gain admission to
a working Castle, or the room of any K. G C., give 11 (one distinct rap) at the door.   The Sentinel on duty will then raise the
wicket and demand the countersign, which is 12, (SOLDIERS,
always lettered except at Castle door.)   You will then pass to
the center of the room and give the true sign of the K. G. C.: it
is 13, (left hand on heart; right hand raised.)   This will be recognized by a bow from the Captain, when you will at once take
your seat.   The sign of assent is 14, (both hands up;) of dissent
15, (one hand up;) the grip is 16, (press with thumb one inch
above second knuckle;) the token 17, (Golden Circle encasing
block hands closed on scroll; the whole to be the size of a dime)
Every member may wear the sign of his degree. ,

And now, reader, you know as much about the signs, grips,
tokens, &c., of the Knights of the Golden Circle as they themselves do.   We may here remark that the initiation fee for the
First Degree is one dollar, for the Second five dollars, for the
Third ten.

From the Second or Financial Degree we need give but little.
The following is the closing part of the initiation :

Captain.   The head quarters of this organization are at 23,
(Monterey) where most of the stores and munitions are depos-

ited. The Financial Head quarters are at ——; Col. N. J. Scott is at present Financial Chairman.   *   *   *

Inspector.   *   *   *

Lieutenant.   *   *   *

Captain. I shall now give you the unwritten parts of this work, and I trust you will be careful in its use. If a general war ensues, we shall dispense with the First Degree, and rely on this and the Third.

Name—18 (True Faith:) sign—25 (fore finger and thumb of right hands joined, while with the rest of the hand upon the right eye is touching with the middle finger,) answer—26 (same with left hand and left eye:) password 27 (Monterey:) night word of distress—32 (St. Mary:) response—31 and say 5 (grasp by wrist and say Rio Grande;) emblem—28 (gold circle encasing Greek cross, in center of which is star.) This is the 29 (key) to our 30 (secret alphabet:) use of 33 (K. G. C.) 56 (George Bickley:) guard sign ½ 28 (gold circle encasing Greek cross, in center of which is a star;) silence 25 (forefinger and thumb of right hand joined, while with the rest of the hand open the right eye is touching on middle finger) on lips; danger—right—same with left.

And now it remains for us to give the Ritual of the Third Degree, which, as being the most important, we shall publish almost entire. We have not the time or space for commenting on it now. Every citizen can judge of it for himself. The Roman Catholics, and the foreign born population will see how they are proscribed by this mysterious Order: this central and guiding power of the secession and disunion party. All will see, too, that the Order declares for a Monarchy, a Limited Monarchy, as they call it, until all their purposes in regard to Mexico shall have been accomplished, and we need not suggest how brief will be the period within which, if they get their *Limited* Monarchy, they will make it an *Absolute* Monarchy.

THIRD OR POLITICAL DEGREE OF THE 33 (K. G. C.)—NAMED 57 (Knights of the Columbian Star.)

INSTRUCTIONS: Officers of the Council shall be a Governor and a Secretary. Every 57 (Knight of the Columbian Star) is qualified to act in either capacity.

Qualifications for Membership.

Candidate must be familiar with the work of the two former Degrees; must have been born in 58 (a Slave State,) or if in 59 (a Free State,) he must be a citizen; 60 (a Protestant) and 61 (a Slaveholder.) A candidate who was born in 58 (a Slave State) need not be 61 (a Slaveholder) provided he can give 62 (Evidences of character as a Southern man.)

Object: To form a council for the 33 (K. G. C.) and to organize 63 (a government) for 2 (Mexico.) No 57 (Knight of the Columbian Star) shall admit, except to a brother 57, that he has this Degree, for reasons that will hereafter appear. Any two 57s can confer the degree on others, the oldest 57 acting as Governor.

Council Hall.   *   *   *

APPROACHING CANDIDATES —Of course all 33 (K. G. C.) know each other. There being two 57 in hailing distance of the court house of said county—that is, 64 (within the county,) they will confer together as to the worthiness of any 33, whom they may think a proper person to be made a 57, and, having agreed, one or both of them will go to the person, each knowing the other 's a 33, and tell him that there is a gentleman 64 (within the county) who has the power to confer the Third Degree, and propose to him that all three shall, or more, if so the case is, go and apply for it—telling him or them, at the same time, that the fee will be 65 (ten dollars.) If he assents, propose a time and place, and be punctual. Let it not be exactly the place where the degree is to be conferred, but near. The 57 (Knights of the Columbian Star) act as if *they* also sought the Degree. Also, tell the candidate that, as he or you may be rejected, it will be expected that he will not mention the matter to any one till the result is known.

When in the room, the Governor will take the Bible, and will cause all to lay their hands thereon, when each will repeat after the Governor the following:

INITIATION.

We three, (or any other number, as the case may be,) citizens of 58, (a Slave State) do hereby and herein, in the presence of each other and the Great Jehovah, solemnly and sincerely pledge our faith and honor to conceal and never reveal to any mortal being, save such as we know to be 57, (Knights of the Columbian Star,) any circumstance or thing that may here transpire during the next hour, and to keep the knowledge of this hour forever secret from all but 57. In the name of God. Amen!

[All take seats.]

SECRETARY. What are you that you are thus leading off in this work, with which you seem so familiar?

GOVERNOR. I am, what you are, a 57; you being the Secretary and I the Governor of this Council, and I here promise to conscientiously do my duty at all times while I hold fellowship with the 33. But, sir, will you explain why it was necessary to proceed as we have?

SECRETARY. We thus proceed because the laws of the Order demand it, and because the Order will lose its efficiency as soon as it ceases to be absolutely secret. It is not permitted that we shall be known to any person living, except to those who are 57. You will find nothing in the Order of which to be ashamed. Not even the 33 must know who has this Degree. This is, perhaps, the only real secret order in the World. *It must be kept secret!*

GOVERNOR. [To Candidate.] I have a few questions to ask you, which I trust you will answer without reserve, for I pledge you my word as a man, as a 57, and as Governor of this Council, that I am in earnest in this work, and would not have sought you out, unless I had thought this whole work would meet your unqualified approbation.

1. Give me the sign, password and grip of a 1 (Knight of the Iron Hand,)
2. Give me the signs, password and grip of a 18 (True Faith.)

3. To what 66 (Castle) do you belong?
4. Where were you born?
5. Where was your father and mother born?
6. Are you 60 (a Protestant) or 67 (a Roman Catholic?)
7. Where do you now live?
8. Do you belong to any other secret society?
9. Married or single?
10. Are you 61 (a Slaveholder?)
11. Will you stand firm in your obligation to the 33 (K G C.?)
12. Do you believe in the religion of Jesus Christ?
13. Are you willing to help in spreading it?

SECRETARY. Judging from what you have seen of the 33 Project, and by what you know of us, are you now willing to be united with us in a society from which you can never resign, but which can in no way compromise you, since the only work and responsibilities we put on you are these:

1. Secrecy as to who the 57 are.
2. To attend every call of a Council made by the Governor General of this State.
3 To do for every brother what every brother has sworn to do for you.
4. To inform the nearest working brother known to you, of danger to the 33 or 57.
5. To exercise a cautious prudence in counteracting false impressions of the 33, and to report to 56, (George Bickley) or his successor or successors, any improper or dangerous actions you may know of.
6. To respond to the call of any 1 rother in your country.
7. And never to speak of the work and character of this degree of the 33 to any one except 57, only as you express sentiments taught by the Order.

We shall not force you to work unless you desire to do so, but on the call of five brothers you must respond, if in your power so to do. Once a 57, (Knight of the Columbian Star) so you will live and die, though no mortal man may know it but 57.

GOVERNOR. Are you willing to proceed?

[Candidate answers, yes.]

SECRETARY. Every knee shall bend to God, and every tongue confess his name.

GOVERNOR. Brothers, we will kneel for prayer. * * *

GOVERNOR. Mr. Secretary, collect the fees of this [or these] candidates, and we will proceed in the work of initiation.

OBLIGATION DELIVERED BY GOVERNOR.

Before God and these witnesses, I do vow that I will never reveal the signs, grips, passwords, tokens or significants of the 57, (Knights of the Columbian Star) to any man, woman or child, except to a 57 in good and lawful standing, and then only as hereafter directed, and for the lawful purposes of this Order And I pledge and commit myself fully and freely to each of the following obligations, and in perfect g od faith:

1st. I vow and promise to conceal the names of the 57, the objects and character thereof, and never to speak of the same as though I was a member, except to those who can give me our sacred word in such a way as to satisfy me they are 57.

2d. No matter what secrets may be given to me by a 57, if given as the secret of a 57 and because I am one, I will hold the same sacredly in my own knowledge, and never recommunicate it, even to a 57, (Knight of the Columbian Star) unless authorized so to do by the brother whose secret it is. I will never speak evil of a brother 57, either before his face or behind his back. I will never dishonor the wife or daughter of a 57, I knowing them to be such, but I will shield and protect the character of all 57 whom I may know to be such, their wives, daughters and families.

3d. I will oppose, to the utmost of my ability, and never consent, but vote against the admission of any confirmed drunkard, professional gambler, rowdy, convict. felon, 68, (Abolitionist.) negro, Indian, minor, idiot or 69, (Foreigner,) to membership in this department of the 33, but I will get as many good and eligible 70 (Southern born men) to join this Degree as I can.

4th. * * *
5th. * * *

6th. I do promise and vow that I will use my best exertions to find out any and every 68 (Abolitionist) in my county, whether 71 (man, woman or child,) and forward the name of such to 56, (George Bickley) or his lawful successor, or, in case I remain in the 72 (United States) after 56 and the 33 have gone to the 2, (Mexico) I will report the same to the Governor-General of this State, and I will keep a close watch on all such, and report at every meeting of my Council, for the information of the 57 remaining in the 72 (United States.) If I know of any 68 who is a 73 (stranger or traveler) trading with 100 (negroes) or doing any other unlawful act I will at once inform all 57 in my country—shall call the 57 to meet in Council, that proper steps may be taken for 74 (his exposure.)

7th. If any 75 (insurrection) shall be started, and it comes to my knowledge, I will do all I have promised above. Or should my State or any other 76, (Southern State) be 77 ('nvaded) by 68, (Abolitionists) I will muster the largest force I can, and go to the scene of danger, if well and able to go. I further promise to do all I can to build up a public sentiment in my State favorable to 18. (the expulsion of free negroes,) that they may be sent to 2 (Mexico.) I further promise that no 79 (free negro) shall marry 80, (my slave) or 80 marry a 79, if I can prevent it.

8th. I also promise to report to the Gove' nor-General of the State the names of all 67 (Roman Catholic) ministers in my county, as well as of all 31 (Northern teachers,) and no 69 (foreigners) or 68 (Abolitionists) shall ever receive this degree if I can prevent it—one negative vote only being necessary to reject any one from receiving this Degree, which vote must be taken before the candidate has been approached.

9th. I will protect and defend all widows and orphans, to the best of my ability, and especially those of a 57, and I vow I will never desert the 57, or their cause and aims, while three members remain and consent to propagate it. And, should they succeed in 82 (conquering and Southernizing) the whole or any part of 2 (Mexico) I will do all I can to prevent any 67 (Roman Catholic) from being appointed to any office of profit or trust, and even in the 72 (U S.) I will always give the preference to 60 (a Protestant,) and especially to 57. I will do all I can, as an honorable man, to make 55 (a Slave State) of 2. As such, I will urge its 83 (annexation) to 72, (U. S.) otherwise I will oppose it with equal zeal. In 2 I will endeavor to cause to be opened to the public all 84 (nunneries, monasteries or convents) and there shall be no advantages to 67 (Roman Catholic) which is not equally accorded to 60 (Protestant.) The 50 (Bible) shall be adopted for use in all public schools, and any 85 (Priest) who shall be detected in 86 (gambling, or violating the ordinances of religion,) shall be expelled from 2. Any minister holding any place under the Government must be 60 (Protestant.)

10th. All civil places of prominence shall be given, so far as my influence goes, to 57, (Knights of the Columbian Star) and, when these are supplied, to the 18 (True Faith;) then to the 1 (Knights of the Iron Hand.) I will advocate the establishment of 63 (a Government,) which shall place the power in the hands of the most educated and moral, and oppose the recognition of any 87 (Negro, Mulatto, Indian or mixed blood,) to citizenship. I will sustain the effort to reduce the 88 (Peon system) to 89 (Perpetual Slavery,) and to divide them to 1, (Knights of the Iron Hand,) 18, (True Faith,) and 57, (Knights of the Columbian Star,) in the proportion of 1, 2, 3, to have and hold forever. But the same laws shall be enacted for their protection as are recognized in every other 58 (Slave State.)

11th. Until the whole civil, political, financial and religious reconstruction of 2 (Mexico) has been completed, I will recognize a 90 (Limited Monarchy) as the best form of 63 (Government) for the purpose in view, since it can be made strong and effective.

12th. To prevent the entrance of any 68 (Abolitionist) into 2 (Mexico,) I will sustain a passport system, and any and every 73 (stranger or traveler) shall go before the customs officer at the port of his entry, and there take an oath, stating whether he intends to become a citizen, and, if so, that he will sustain and support the government then in existence, and that he will not interfere with the system of 89 (perpetual slavery) then recognized, but that he will obey the laws then recognized. If he be a traveler merely, he shall give up his passport to the Chief of Police on his entrance into each town, and which shall be returned to him on demand of the same officer, when about to leave for another place. And any 73 who shall pass, or attempt to pass, without a passport, shall be arrested and expelled from the country, and upon resistance he shall be shot; but every traveler so entering 2 (Mexico) must be informed of this rule.

13th. The successor to 56 (Geo. Bickley) must be over thirty years of age, of Southern birth, liberally educated, a 57, (Knight of the Columbian Star,) sound of body and mind, and married, and 60 (a Protestant.) He shall swear to carry out this policy, and to extend 91 (slavery) over the whole of 92, (Central America,) if in his power. He shall try to acquire 93 (Cuba,) and control 94 (the Gulf of Mexico.) No one else will I sustain. But for such a one, who must be proposed by the 95 (Cabinet

Minister,) and elected by all 57, or a majority of them, I will sustain here, there, or elsewhere. When the 33 (K. G. C.) cross the 5, (Rio Grande,) I will do all I can to send in £6, (recruits for the army,) and, if I should ever cease to be an active worker for the 57, I will keep secret what I know of the real character of the organization, and I promise never to confer this degree in any other way than in the way I have here received it, and I will forward to £6, (George Bickley,) or to the Governor General of this State, the name and fees of every candidate whom I shall initiate as Governor. In witness, I do voluntarily, here in these presence, sign my name and P. O. Address. (Governor asks, "will you sign?")

SECRETARY. Perhaps you had better hear the whole degree and then sign, for, unless we have your entire approbation, we do not wish to commit you to anything. I am well aware that this whole scheme is a bold and daring one, that can but surprise you at first, as it did me, and for this reason I beg to state a few facts for your consideration. In the rise and progress of Democracy in America, we have seen its highest attainment. In the very outset, it was based on high religious principles, and adopted as a refuge from despotism. In the North, Puritanism melted it, and went so far as to leave out the natural conservative element of all Democracies, 97, (domestic slavery.) As a result, we have presented now, social, religious and political anarchy. From Millerism and spiritualism, every Utopian idea has numerous advocates, The manufacturer is an aristocrat, while the working man is a serf. The latter class, constantly goaded by poverty, seek a change, they care not what it may be. Democracy, unrestrained by 97, (domestic slavery,) multiplies the manufacturing classes indefinitely, but it debases the mechanic. Whoever knew a practical shoemaker, or a maker of pinheads, to have a man's ambition? They own neither land or property, and have no tie to the institutions of the country. The Irishman emigrates, and the Frenchman remains at home. The one hates his country, the other adores his. The Frenchman is a slaveholder and a man. The Irishman is a serf and an outcast. The South is naturally agricultural, and the farmer being most of the time in the midst of his growing crops, seeing the open operation of nature, his mind expands, he grows proud and ambitious of all around, and feels himself a man. He wants no change, either in civil, political or religious affairs. He cultivates the soil, and it yields him the means to purchase labor. He becomes attached to home and its associations, and remains forever a restrained Democrat, restrained by moral and civil law from any and all overt acts. He needs and makes a centralized government, because his property is at stake when anarchy prevails.

GOVERNOR. Now, in the case of 2 (Mexico;) suppose we were to elevate to citizenship 87, (Negro, mulatto, Indian or mixed blood,) do you not see at once that the very act would undo all the results of 82 (conquering and Southernizing?) We should be voted back to 72 (U. S.) the day of the first election. None but white 89 (landholders) should be allowed the exercise of the citizen's franchise. These are the men who pay the taxes and guard the people. Again, efficient officers require experience, which can only be acquired by time, hence, places should be held as long as the holder can discharge faithfully and efficiently his functions.

SECRETARY. You will therefore see that we labor not only for the extension of 97 (Domestic Slavery) in 2, but that we seek to make 63 (a government) strong enough to protect and perpetuate it. The means for erecting a 90 (Limited Monarchy) are in 2. They only require to be used well. We require a vast number of officers, some thousands in all. Now, help us make 63, (a government,) and go you and send your son and let him take his place. The work is large, and there are plenty of us to do it. Of course the whole scheme must be managed well. As soon as everything is reduced to order, then we may canvass the question of a republic.

GOVERNOR. Vast sums will be needed. 2 can furnish every dollar. The day we cross 5, (Rio Grande,) parties in 99 (Matamoras) will advance us $1,000,000, and others at 23 (Monterey) $2,000,000. The revenue of those two places amounts to $7,000,000, and the other cities in 24 (Northern Mexico) very large sums. The 33 then is only a repetition of the East India Co., or the Hudson Bay Co. You are now a stockholder. Help us to get in the field with your money and your influence: help us to procure material, for you are as much interested as any of us. Money will follow our success. We shall concentrate in 20 (Encinal Co., Texas) by Sept. 15th, 1860, (a misprint, we presume, for 1861.—ED. JOURNAL.) and we will cross 5 (Rio Grande) by the 1st day of 6 (October.) Now, sir, if you will be one of us, either to go or to stay at home, you will sign your name as all of us have done, after which I will give you the Ceremonial of this Degree. [*Candidate signs at the end of the work; and he also signs his own work.*]

SECRETARY. The signs, test signs, words and passwords, grips and pass-grips, tokens and keys of this degree must be well learned, for on their proper use depends your standing in this Order. Notice them, practice them, and heed them.

[The candidate is here made to sign the obligation, as also a copy for himself. When he has done this, present him with a copy and a key of the Degree.]

SIGNS, &c.—(These are now to be given in full and explained.) ☞ See Key.

[The key here mentioned we have. We will give it in such a form that the reader will understand it. The sign is *a* [raise hat with left hand over right, open hand on top of head.] The countersign is *b* [left hand with hat extended to right angles, hand by side.] The silent sign is *c* [left hand on back of head.] The answer is *d* [right hand on forehead, then extended.] The night sign is *e* [two distinct claps of hands, and repeat once.] The test sign is *f* [finger and thumb of left hand take hold of lip.] The sacred word is *g* [Eloi.] The password is *h* [Andalusia,] and to this is added, in parenthesis, "Notice instructions in use of words." The night word given with *e* is *i* [high.] The grip is *j* [as given.] The pass grip is *k* [same with left hand, still holding by right.] The token or emblem is *l* [same as shown.] The answer to *f* is *m* [right thumb and fore finger on pit of stomach.]

That's all we have at present to give, and, as we have said, it may be relied on as authentic. It is a revelation of the mysteries of an Order which claims to be, and no doubt is, powerful in our land. Its emissaries have lured into it thousands of young men, by impressing them with utterly false ideas of its nature and designs. The members of the First and Second degrees know nothing of the Third, although they are unwittingly guided and controlled by it. Let them examine the revolting character of the obligations of the Third Degree, and then make all haste to repudiate an organization that deserves the scorn and abhorrence of all just men.

The reader will remark that General Bickley insists, in his circular, that "it is exceedingly desirable and important 'to organize the State of Kentucky before the August elections." No doubt the intention of the Order is to make its power felt in various ways on the day of the election. We look forward with no little interest to the result.

The Roman Catholics and foreign born citizens will find much in the Ritual of the Third Degree deserving their attention. Irishmen in particular will meet with something interesting to themselves.

If public opinion has not utterly lost its virtue, it will speedily sweep this miserable Order off the face of this earth. Will Geo. Bickley dare, after the exposition, to show his face among men? Will any Knight of the Golden Circle have the audacity to avow himself one, or let himself be known as one? Is it true, can it be true, that men of respectable standing in our community acknowledge, either before the world or in their own hearts, the obligations of the Third Degree of this infamous association?

The K. G. C.'s declare for a Limited Monarchy, and say that it will be time enough to discuss the question of a Republic when all the extraordinary purposes that they propose to themselves shall have been accomplished.

The K. G. C.'s of the Third Degree, it seems, look keenly to office. They require that *all* the members of their Degree shall have offices before any member of the Second Degree can be accommodated, and that *all* the members of the Second Degree shall be provided with offices before a solitary individual of the First can be accommodated. But then they say that they are going to have thousands of offices, and they mean that the incumbents of offices shall hold on for life.

It is no wonder that the members of the Third Degree, Knights of the Columbian Star, as they call themselves, guard carefully in their Ritual against ever being known as such, even to their brethren of the First and Second Degrees.

Let all bear steadily in mind that the Order of the Knights of the Golden Circle is now and has all along been the central sun of the Secession party of Kentucky.